Sisters

Also in the Contents series

Contents

Sisters

Stories edited by Miriam Hodgson

Mammoth

First published in Great Britain 1998
by Mammoth, an imprint of Reed International Books Limited
Michelin House, 81 Fulham Road, London SW3 6RB

ISBN 0 7497 2982 1

10 9 8 7 6 5 4 3 2 1

A CIP catalogue record for this title
is available from the British Library

Typeset by Avon Dataset Ltd, Bidford on Avon, B50 4JH
Printed in Great Britain by Cox & Wyman Ltd, Reading, Berkshire

CONTENTS

A Close Match

Helen Dunmore

'Oh – is she really your sister?' People are always asking me that, as if I'd bother to lie. And then they look from me to Jennifer. 'I'd never have guessed you were sisters.'

Nor would I. I used to make up a lot of stuff about being adopted, and that was why Mum and Jennifer were tall and fair, and I was short and dark. But my dad's dark, or at least he was before he went grey, and he's half a head shorter than Mum.

'It's funny how different sisters can be, isn't it?' That's what my aunts and uncles say. But it's not all that funny for me, because the difference is that Jennifer's got everything. She has long legs that go deep brown in summer, and thick smooth hair that gets blonde streaks in it. She's one of those people who always look right. And she's easy to be with. She doesn't get prickly and hurt and bad-tempered. She doesn't fall out with people. She doesn't get into rages when Mum asks her about homework, or slam her door and knock her best pottery elephant off the shelf and smash it. Jennifer's always done her homework. Sheet after sheet of it, in her beautifully neat round handwriting, handed in on time. Her marks are always good enough, but not too good. Nobody calls Jennifer a keener.

And then there are Jennifer's clothes. Mum's always saying, 'I give each of you girls exactly the same clothes allowance. Can you please tell me, Kim, why you never have anything to wear?' Yes, Mum, I can tell you. Because I bought those jeans which would only have fitted me if I'd grown about four inches taller and four inches slimmer. Because I didn't read the care label on my new red top, which was the best thing I ever bought – even Jennifer wanted to borrow it. When it came out of the machine it was a sad red rag, and the two white towels I'd put in with it were sad pink rags. Mum made me pay for them, because they were new, so that was another twenty pounds, and now, surprise, surprise, I haven't got anything to wear. Jennifer doesn't spend much on clothes, but she always looks fantastic.

'Where did you get that skirt, Jennifer?'

'Oh, it was in the sale at River Island. It was only four pounds ninety nine. It was the last one.'

The last one. Of course.

Jennifer does gymnastics, and she's in the school netball team and the school tennis team. I love watching her play tennis. She seems to know just where the ball's going to go, and she's suddenly there with her racket, ready to hit it back. I asked her once how she did it, but she frowned and said, 'I don't know.' She doesn't even care about winning. If she loses she just shrugs and says, 'It was a nice game, anyway.'

But Jennifer hasn't been playing much tennis this summer. I wanted to book a court yesterday, but she said, 'Not today, Kim. I don't feel like it.' She lay sprawled on the grass, with a book beside her which she wasn't reading.

'Are you OK?' I asked. She nodded, and picked up the book and pretended to read it again. She didn't look that great. Later on I was playing CDs in my room when I heard Mum's voice. She sounded really angry. Angry? With Jennifer? I opened the door a crack, and listened.

'I don't ask you to do much, Jennifer, but I don't expect to come in from work and find you haven't cleared the kitchen. You may be on holiday, but I'm not.

I expect to have to chase after Kim when it's her turn, but not you.'

She was really shouting. I shut the door. I could feel a little secret grin curling over my face. A little later I heard Jennifer clattering the dishes, and the water gushing in the sink.

Things went on like that for a while. It was different from every other holiday. Jennifer didn't go out. When her friends rang she said she was busy. After a while they stopped ringing so much. She lay out on the grass day after day, with a book or a magazine or her Walkman.

Sometimes she fell asleep for hours. It was so boring. When Mum came home she'd ask what we'd been doing and I'd say I'd been round to Katie's, or I'd been making chocolate brownies or whatever. Jennifer wouldn't say anything. She'd drift upstairs, looking as if she still had the sun in her eyes. Once I came out of the kitchen and I saw her standing halfway up the stairs, quite still, holding onto the banister and staring at nothing.

I thought it was going to go on for ever. Jennifer never even asked what I was doing. I could have done anything I wanted, all those long, hot holidays. But suddenly everything changed. I'd been swimming with Katie and Lisa, but they were going off to have lunch at Burger King and I hadn't any money, so I came home alone. It was very hot and there was hardly anyone out on the streets. I went in through our back garden gate, and there was Jennifer as usual, sprawled on her back in the sun. But there was something about the way she was lying which was different. And her face looked wrong. It was a dirty-washing-up-water colour.

'Jennifer? *Jennifer!*' She didn't answer. She didn't move. I dropped my stuff on the grass and ran to her. My heart was banging and my fingers were sweaty. I had a horrible feeling that she wasn't ever going to answer. I bent down and shook her shoulder. Then her eyes opened and she looked at me.

'Are you OK? What's happened?'

'I feel funny. I think I fainted. Kim, get Mum.'

'Mum's at work.'

Jennifer tried to sit up. Her hair was dark with sweat and it stuck to her forehead. She looked awful, as if she was going to be sick.

'Kim, get Mum,' she said again, as if she hadn't understood about Mum being at work.

'OK. I won't be a minute. Listen, just stay there, Jennifer, all right?' I ran across the grass to the kitchen door. If I used the kitchen phone I could still see Jennifer. She looked so bad. She looked . . .

'Mum! Mum, it's Jennifer . . .'

That was the beginning. After that it was like a tide coming in. You think you've got plenty of time, because the water's only up to your knees. Then you're thigh-deep, and the waves are pushing you hard. Suddenly the sea's all around you, and then between one wave and the next you lose your footing and when you reach down there's nothing, only deep, cold water. No matter how hard you struggle towards land, you can't get there again.

Everything changed. Mum took Jennifer to the doctor that same evening because she still looked so awful.

'It's probably nothing, but we'll just get you checked over.' And she must have phoned Dad, because he came home early too, and cooked fried chicken with rice and peas, and made a lot of jokes which didn't really hide the way either of us felt when surgery time was long over and Jennifer and Mum still didn't come back.

Jennifer was having tests. That's why they'd been so long. Mum looked pale, too.

'What kind of tests?' I asked Jennifer when Mum went upstairs to change.

'Oh. Blood and stuff. He looked at my legs.'

'Looked at your legs? What's wrong with your legs?'

'They've got all –' she paused, 'bruises on them.'

'Did somebody hit you? Is that what's wrong?'

Jennifer smiled, very faintly. ''Course not. They just came.'

She was wearing her white jeans. Suddenly I realised she'd been wearing jeans or a long cotton skirt for about two weeks. Never her shorts or her swimsuit, even though she was always lying in the sun.

'Show me.'

Jennifer hesitated. Then she took a quick look at the door to be sure it was shut, and unzipped her jeans. 'There.'

There were dark, splotchy bruises on her thighs. She looked down at them, then quickly at me. She looked almost . . . pleading. As if there was something she wanted me to say.

'They're not so bad,' I said. 'It was worse when you fell off your bike.'

'Yes,' said Jennifer quickly. 'Yes, it was, wasn't it.' And she did up her jeans again, looking relieved.

The next thing was that Jennifer had to go to hospital for more tests. The blood tests hadn't been too clear or something. Mum and Dad went too, but when they came back Jennifer wasn't with them.

'We dropped her off at Martina's,' said Mum. 'Peel some potatoes for me, would you, Kim?' She went out of the room and I heard her going upstairs, nearly as slowly as Jennifer had done. I peeled the potatoes, then I thought I'd go up and get my CD player so I could listen to music while I laid the table.

Mum's door was open. I just glanced in, the way you do. I wasn't trying to look or anything. Mum was lying on the bed, her face in her pillow. Dad was sitting beside her, with his arms round her as much as he could. They weren't saying anything, but Mum's back was shaking and I could tell she was crying. I went into my room really quickly and grabbed the CD player and went downstairs.

Jennifer came back very late and went straight to her room. I knocked and after a long time she said, 'Come in.' Then she looked at me and said, 'Oh. It's you.'

I fiddled with her light switch. 'Are you OK, Jennifer? I mean, were the tests all right and everything?'

Jennifer gave me the coldest, hardest look she had ever given me. 'Don't be stupid,' she said. I felt myself flush red all over, as if I'd done something wrong.

'How can the tests be OK,' went on Jennifer in the same voice, 'when they're to find out if I've got leukaemia and I'm probably going to die?'

Jennifer did have leukaemia. Mum and Dad told me. But it didn't mean Jennifer was going to die. The treatment for leukaemia was amazing these days. Most people recovered. I sat there while Mum and Dad told me all the hopeful things about leukaemia, and I thought of Mum lying on the bed crying, and I knew she'd guessed too, before the test results came back, just like Jennifer had.

It was a few weeks later that Mum came into my room when I was in bed, just before I fell asleep. I knew all sorts of other stuff by then, that I didn't want to know, about white cells counts and what was normal and what was Jennifer. Mum and Dad said they'd decided to be completely open with me. Jennifer was going to need a lot of treatment but it was going to work. She'd spent a lot of time in hospital already. The only thing Jennifer said was, 'If my hair falls out, I'm not going to wear a wig.' Then she wouldn't talk about any of it any more.

Mum sat on my bed and crossed her legs. It was nearly dark, but I could just about see her face looking at mine.

'Jennifer needs more treatment,' she said. 'Dr Aitchison's told us he thinks the best therapy for her at this stage is a bone marrow transplant.' That was the way Mum talked then, just like a doctor herself.

'A bone marrow transplant.'

'Yes. You see, if Jennifer could receive some healthy bone marrow which can make new cells for her, she'd have a good chance of making a complete recovery.'

'How can she? I mean, she can't have other people's bones transplanted.'

Mum sighed, as if I was being deliberately thick. And

maybe I was. The whole thing was so horrible I didn't even want to understand it.

'Just the marrow,' she said. 'They can take it out of a healthy person's bones, and put it into Jennifer's.'

'How?' I asked faintly. Mum hesitated.

'The thing is,' she said, 'the bone marrow has to be a very close match to Jennifer's. It's no good just anybody being a donor, or her body will reject it. But people in a family are often a very close match. So Dad and I are going to be tested to see if we're good enough . . .' She was silent for a while, then she added, in a brisk voice as if she was asking me to do the washing-up, 'But the best chance of a match is from a sibling.'

A sibling. I heard the word as if it was just a word, then I understood. 'You mean – a sister?'

'Yes, Kim, there's a very good chance that your marrow might be a close enough match.'

My bone marrow! I felt completely sick. 'You mean – take out my bone marrow and give it to Jennifer?'

'Not all of it, don't be silly, Kim. Just a little bit.'

I notice what Mum doesn't say, as well as what she does. I noticed that she didn't say, *It won't hurt.*

'What do they do?'

'Well, they give you an anaesthetic of course, so it's just like going to sleep.'

'What do they do, Mum?'

'It's quite a simple operation. They just take some marrow from your bone – from your hipbone, it'd be – while you're asleep.'

'What with? A needle?'

'Well – yes. A sort of needle. Dr Aitchison said he'd be happy to talk it over with you, if you've got any questions.'

You bet I have, I thought, but I didn't say anything. I hate hospitals, I hate illness, I hate needles and above all I hate doctors explaining things to me as if I'm about two years old.

'It may not happen. You may not be a close enough match,' said Mum.

'No,' I said. 'After all, look how different we are. People are always saying we don't look like sisters.'

But we weren't as different as everybody thought. The tests showed that Jennifer and I were more alike than anyone had ever believed. I saw Mum's face go shaky with relief, and Dad turned away and whistled through his teeth, because that was what he did when he couldn't handle us seeing how he felt. Then Mum and Dad were both looking at me. It was a strange, strange feeling. I wanted to say, *Take it away. Don't make it have to happen*. But I knew it was too late for that. Only Jennifer didn't react. She didn't look pleased or anything. She looked as if she was thinking about something else.

Jennifer had to have a lot of treatment to get her ready for the bone marrow transplant. She was in a little room on her own and I wasn't allowed to go in, because of infection getting to her. There was glass at the end wall and I used to wave to her and hold up little notes, but she didn't look terribly interested.

'She's very tired,' said Mum. 'It's the chemotherapy. Better leave her to rest now.' But I noticed that one time when Martina came with us, Jennifer sat right up on her bed and wrote little notes back to Martina. The next day she didn't want to see anyone, not even Mum.

'She's worried about her hair,' said Mum. Later on, in the car, I pulled my scrunchy off and my hair flopped round my face, as it always did. I tried to imagine what it would be like if it started falling out when I combed it. I tried to imagine a wig, but I couldn't.

But the next day Jennifer wouldn't see me again, and I stopped feeling sorry for her.

'She's such a bitch!' I said to Dad in the car on the way back. He didn't say anything.

'Why should I have holes in my bones and get my bone marrow sucked out, just for a bitch like her who won't even talk to me?' I thought Dad would be angry with me, but he just met my eyes in the driving mirror. 'I can't give you a reason,' he said.

And now I'm in hospital. It's horrible. They've given me something which has dried up my mouth, and I haven't had anything to drink, and I'm really hungry. And there are people clattering about the whole time, and talking to me as if I'm an idiot. And I still haven't seen Jennifer.

And I'm frightened. I wonder if Jennifer's frightened too? She's waiting, all prepared, just as I am, so that as soon as they take my bone marrow it can go into her. And then, maybe, my healthy cells will take root in her and start to grow. After a while they won't be my cells any more, they'll be hers. They'll start making healthy blood for her, the way they should have done all along.

I can hear wheels skidding and squeaking on the lino. I know if I look up I'll see a trolley coming, and yet more people with J-cloth caps over their heads and big smiles on their faces. This time they haven't come to check on me or chat to me. They've come to wheel me away.

I think of the bruises on Jennifer's legs. I think of her hair. Mum says she shuts her eyes when she combs her hair in the morning. Then she says she doesn't care, she isn't going to wear a wig anyway. People will just have to accept her the way she is. And Mum says, *They will*.

Just imagine, I'm a closer match to Jennifer than even Mum or Dad. But when you think of it, that's the way it ought to be. Your mum and dad get old and die, while you've still got a lot of your life left to live. But your sister doesn't die. She grows up, and goes to work, and maybe gets married, and has kids, and grows old, just the way you do. Your sister stays alive as long as you do, till you're two scrunched-up little old ladies together, laughing at the things you used to do when you were little. *Two old ladies*. Are you listening, Jennifer?

But it doesn't matter if you're listening or not. It doesn't even matter if you don't want to see me. We're as close a match as you can get, and there's nothing in the world either of us can do about it.

The Winter Sister

Jenny Nimmo

She came from the snow and vanished into it. She was a gift from my father but I never thanked him.

That Christmas I had tried to recreate the atmosphere our mother always managed to achieve; the mysterious blend of enchantment, sanctity and anticipation; the smells and flavours of pine, spice, stored fruit and burning tallow. Our mother loved the forest and at Christmas-time she carried it into our home. She filled the house with branches of evergreen, sugared fruit and mellow, glittering light.

In the spring of 1913 our mother died. A fever was

15

raging in the village and she wanted to bring relief to the suffering and the dying. Our father begged her to keep safe within the walls of his estate, but he couldn't always watch her. He owned land a hundred miles away, Polish woods that bordered Eastern Prussia, and he had to visit his estates. As soon as he left, our mother put on her stout leather boots and carried a basket of fresh linen down to the tall gates that opened on to the road. And then she walked almost a mile to the village, where she worked all day, changing linen and praying with the dying. I saw none of this, for she forbade me to follow her. I heard it from my brother, Peter, who wouldn't heed her warning and secretly shadowed her. Perhaps he thought he could protect her in some way. He is a better person than I.

Nothing could protect her. She made a second visit, and when she returned she sat in the hall, fanning herself and dabbing her cheeks with a handkerchief. She said she felt a little faint, but when she saw our anxious faces, she smiled and told us it was nothing. She was tired and would take a rest before the evening meal. She never left her bed again. In two days she was dead.

I thought I would never forgive my mother for bringing that terrible death on herself. But Peter's grief was worse than mine. He cried all day and wouldn't be consoled. I'm older by two years and stronger.

Our father's sorrow was quiet and deep; expressed by sudden silences, anguished glances at my mother's empty chair and long solitary walks.

'You're the mistress of this house now, Magdalena,' he said one day. 'Your conversation is polite and witty, your manners graceful. You must take your mother's place. Perhaps mine too, for I am lost without her. Sometimes, I feel like a drowning man.'

His words both frightened and pleased me. I was proud of the compliments but dismayed at the prospect of such responsibility. We had a housekeeper, of course, and several servants, and I could turn to my old governess for advice. But without my parents' guidance, how was I to manage?

My mother's absence pressed about me like a shroud. I had shared all my thoughts with her, poured out my dreams, whispered my hopes into her sympathetic ear, laughed and cried with her. Now, I would stand almost motionless for hours, my dreams trapped inside my head, my purpose lost. I think my father was aware of this, and when he took to visiting his estates again, and smiling at the breakfast table, I felt my heart begin to lighten.

They said my father was seeing someone: a General's widow who'd been driven from her home; a Polish noblewoman; a Russian countess who'd gambled away her estate. There were many stories, but I didn't care which was true. My father's sorrows wouldn't drown him after all, and I could be myself again.

Peter asked how I could smile so soon. Shouldn't we still be in mourning? He wouldn't shake off his grief. Not until *she* came – the winter sister.

Autumn passed and December rushed at us. A blizzard swept across the Baltic sea, piling snow against our gates, smothering branches and filling the lane with a wall of ice. The north wind ripped church bells from their towers and flung them, pealing dolefully, into the ice-locked forest. Peter said their helpless chiming was our mother's voice.

I don't believe in ghosts, but to comfort Peter I said that perhaps our mother was sending us a message, and it would please her spirit to see the house filled with pine and spices, and with glittering candles set among green branches, the way she used to do it. It would be our Christmas gift to her.

In mid-December our father had a passage cleared through the snow and set off for his furthest estate. He rode a strong black stallion that could be trusted in the roughest weather. He would be back on the night before Christmas, he told us. There would be presents for everyone, but for me there would be something very special.

Filled with excitement, I laid plans for celebrating the festive season. I plied the cook with questions about pickling and icing. I filled the kitchen with fruit from the storehouse, and begged the servants to drag crates of candles from the cellar. Peter watched my antics with an apathetic, sullen face, and I grew impatient with his misery.

'Our mother's gone,' I cried. 'D'you think it would gladden her to see such gloomy features? Your duty's done. You've mourned enough to satisfy a dozen corpses.'

I'll never forget the tortured look he threw me. 'I can't help it, Magdalena,' he whispered. 'It's all my fault. I could have saved our mother. That day I followed her I saw her take a drink in one of those poor houses. I should have stopped her, but I didn't. I stood at the door, too afraid to go into a room where someone lay dying.'

I wrapped him in my arms and told him that it was no one's fault. My brother had become so thin in the months without our mother, he seemed almost weightless. I told him that she had gone to a better place, and that all she needed was to know that he had forgiven her for leaving us. He must start to enjoy life again.

He said that he would try, and then he asked, almost guiltily, if I could guess what our father would bring home on Christmas eve. 'I mean your gift, Magdalena,' he said, 'your very special surprise.'

I laughed and confessed that I had tried and tried to guess, but still had no idea what the secret gift would be.

Later that day we learnt part of the mystery. A rider came thundering up to our door. He had an urgent message for the count's children, he said. The letter was brought to me in the kitchen where an anxious cook was watching my efforts to turn sugar into caramel.

Our father's message didn't really surprise me, but I felt a little stab of apprehension, a flicker of fear at the sudden uncertainty of life. Also, I suppose, I felt betrayed. I would no longer be mistress of the house, for my father had married again, and would be bringing home a new wife.

Trying to hide my anxiety, I said, 'It's good, isn't it, Peter? For Father and for us. We needed someone to fill our mother's place.'

The look in his blue eyes told me that he knew I held no such sentiments. Silently he shook his head, and then he clasped my hands and held on tightly. We were so close I felt as though we held each other's thoughts. It was the last such moment that we ever shared. If only I had known it then.

We spent the days before Christmas carrying pine cones

and branches of fir into the house. I persuaded my brother to help me, arguing that we would be doing it in our mother's honour, to show the new mistress that her predecessor's inspiration could never be improved on.

Candles were set among the branches, but they were not to be lit until five minutes before my father entered. We covered every table in the hall, the back of every chair. We draped evergreens above the great mirror in the parlour, the lintels and picture-rails. We worked in a kind of breathless frenzy, hopeful but afraid. Eager for our father's arrival, yet anxious of the changes it would bring.

On Christmas eve we sat by the long window in my room. It overlooked the blanket of snow that swept down to the road. A lantern swung from the arch above the open gates. Everything was ready.

They were very late. But we wouldn't leave our post. When my governess called us to supper, we shooed her away. 'Wait! Wait! Wait!' we cried. And she scurried off with a finger pressed to her smiling lips.

We heard the sleigh bells first, ringing across the quiet snow, and my heart began to pound. 'Now?' asked Peter, eager to run for a taper.

'No! No! No!' I cried. 'Not yet. Not until we see them!'

A horse swung through the gates, his coat gleaming

in the lantern-light, dark against the pale snow.

'Now,' I commanded, but as Peter leapt downstairs, I lingered a few seconds and watched the sleigh approach with its huddle of fur-wrapped passengers. I counted no more than two, and then my feet were flying down the wooden staircase, my shaking hand reaching for the tapers that Peter held. Suddenly, the house was alive with excited murmurs, every member of the household held a taper, and as each candle leapt into life, I began to sense my mother's spirit burning fiercely all about me.

The door was opened and I ran to greet my father, but as I stood there, gazing down at the blur of faces, a rush of freezing air thrust me backwards, stealing my breath away. The cold seeped into my bones and I felt my mother's gentle spirit leave our house forever.

'Magdalena!' I was clasped in my father's bear hug, then it was Peter's turn. Behind my father a dark woman walked into the hall. The door was closing and an uncertain movement beyond the woman alerted me; the flurry of a fur coat being shaken, another dark head appearing.

'This is Natalia!' My father's hands on the woman's shoulders, urging her towards us. 'Magdalena, Peter, your new mother.'

We kissed her cool cheek dutifully. She said, 'How beautiful you've made the house,' but she had an empty smile. She would never be our mother. As my father drew her aside, his eyes brimmed with mischievous excitement.

'And this, Magdalena, is your Christmas gift. A sister!'

My ears burned. Disappointment, followed by dismay, washed over me. I was speechless. What had I expected? A trinket? A pearl necklace? A ruby ring? It wasn't the thought of a sister that so repelled me, it was what that sister was.

My father's words seemed muffled and remote. 'Her name is Magda, almost your name . . . Now you must be Lena. Magda and Lena, two halves of a whole name!' His laughter boomed over my head while under my breath I muttered, 'Never, never, never. My name is Magdalena.'

This Christmas gift, this *sister*, was a peasant. A gypsy. I felt tricked, deceived, betrayed. Couldn't my father see what she was? I had never beheld such obviously peasant features. Black hair scraped into an ugly pigtail. Coal-bright eyes glinting in the narrow sockets that slanted above her wide flat cheeks. And she was fat, horribly so, had been reared, most probably, on a diet of bread and pig-fat.

How had it happened? How had Natalia, a Russian noblewoman, produced a peasant child? Later I learned that Magda's father, a colonel, had been killed in the war against Japan. He was a Tartar, a handsome man of outstanding courage and intelligence. But in Magda, all the genes of refinement and beauty had been swept away, in favour of those that marked out the ugliest, most dull-witted, peasant.

She would follow me like a dog, always smiling and seemingly deaf to my insuslts. She would pick up my carelessly mislaid possessions and lay them beside me. She made gifts of clumsy embroidery, she brought cushions for my back, tea when I was thirsty, and I would quickly glance away from the expectant devotion glimpsed in the tilted eyes, rewarding her kindness with unconcealed dislike.

In the weeks that followed, my brother and I amazed each other. Magda drew a laughter from him that I had not heard since our mother died. They tumbled in the snow together, played ridiculous games of hide-and-seek and tag, and ran riot in the icy woods. I could hardly believe the change in Peter, and he, in his turn, seemed to condemn, rather than understand my attitude.

'You're too proud, Lena,' he would taunt. 'Why can't you be nice to our sister?'

'Don't you know?' I would demand.

'No,' he would fling at me before rushing off to find his new companion.

Engrossed with Natalia, my father scarcely noticed

us. But he was fond of Magda, that was clear, and determined to make her part of his family. For her birthday he gave her a crystal horse, and in return she plastered his cheeks with an endless succession of loud kisses.

She put her treasure beside the lamp in her bedroom, where I know she lay and watched it sparkle. I hated this small pleasure of hers. It pursued me day and night. One morning, when she and Peter were outside, I went and took the horse from her room and, leaning on the banisters, twirled it carelessly between my fingers. It slipped out of my hand and fell onto the flagstones in the hall, breaking into a hundred fragments. The sound of shattered crystal was like remote and eerie music.

I was still gazing down at the distant sparkle when she came in. Her cheeks were like shiny red apples, her fat hands pink and sweaty. She knelt and dabbed at the slivers of glass while Peter exclaimed, 'Careful, Magda! What is it?' She knew what it was because, miraculously, the head hadn't shattered.

'I'm sorry,' I called. 'I was taking it to the kitchen to clean it for you and . . .' I shrugged and smiled. 'It was an accident.'

Magda bent her head over the fragments, but Peter shouted, 'Liar,' and something snapped between us.

When spring came I took to visiting my mother's

grave. I went to talk to her. There was no one else. My world had changed and I within it. Hatred and loneliness had made me a stranger to myself. One day, as I stood murmuring to my mother, I felt my arm touched, gently. And there was Magda, right beside me, her fat cheeks swamped with tears. For me. Her pity enraged me.

'Go away!' I screamed. 'I hate you. Don't you understand?'

Her smile died, and I saw a sudden, terrible pain sweep across her dull features. It was gone in a second – a shadow that had never been, and when she walked away she wore her usual stupid grin.

I willed an illness into my bones. I wouldn't eat, wouldn't sleep, took to rambling the woods alone, until, burning with exhaustion I stumbled on the stairs and fell in a helpless bundle onto the stone floor, jarring my brain into senselessness.

What happened after that, I never learned until it was too late. My memories of the fever that engulfed me are like strange dreams. A war broke out in Europe. Armies tramped through our estates, Russian and German. At Tannenberg, not a hundred miles away, three hundred thousand soldiers met, and thousands died, while I drifted in and out of consciousness. I slept for days and woke to pains of indescribable intensity. My only comfort was the quiet presence that roamed my dark room, soothing my head with cool fingers, turning my pillows, wetting my lips with precious water and holding my restless fingers. My mother's spirit, or so I thought. Without it I know I should have died.

The fever broke at last and I woke one morning to find myself surrounded by a sea of faces: my father, Peter, Natalia, my old governess – and Magda. 'Why is she here?' I asked, my eyes focusing on the dark, flat face. As she retreated I saw that she had changed, her face seemed thinner and I noticed that her mother looked at her without affection. All this I caught in a moment of startling precision, a picture that was soon forgotten amidst the attention I received from my elated father. I came to realize how deeply he cared for me, and that the grief he felt at losing my mother would never truly be healed.

I was out of danger but my recovery took several more weeks. I had a broken bone and my muscles had gone to waste. My family took turns in entertaining me as I lay in bed, but Peter's visits were made more out of a sense of duty than affection. He wouldn't look me in the eye, and left as soon as he politely could. I never saw Magda, and couldn't admit to myself that I missed her.

As soon as I was strong enough, my father prepared for the long journey round his estates. This time he took Natalia and they travelled by carriage. The house seemed curiously hollow after they left. Quiet, almost dead. Peter hardly left his room and Magda now took her meals in the kitchen. Sometimes, I would glimpse a shapeless form drift across a dark passage, or see a figure in the woods, sitting hunched on a fallen branch. I was puzzled. Was she avoiding me? I never called out to her.

The snow came early that winter. It fell steadily through the night, and I awoke to an icy silence. I don't know what compulsion led me to my sister's room that morning. I found her standing by her bed, pressing clothes into a battered suitcase.

'What are you doing?' I demanded.

'I'm leaving.' She didn't look at me.

'Leaving? For . . . for what?'

'Forever.'

I wondered if she'd understood my question. 'You can't.' Panic crept into my voice. 'What will your mother say?'

'Nothing. She doesn't like me.'

'Don't be stupid. She's your mother.' I spoke more sharply than I intended.

She shrugged and, like some dreadful automaton, continued her relentless folding and pressing, until she came to the crystal horse-head and, holding it her palm, she murmured, 'Your father brought me here. My mother would have left me.' At last Magda looked at me, and I saw her clearly for the very first time. I saw sagging shoulders, hollow cheeks, a mouth lined by despair and eyes that gave her face a melancholy beauty.

'What will you do?' My voice had become a whisper.

'There's a war on, haven't you heard? An archduke was killed in Sarajevo. I'm a good nurse. They will need me.' It was the longest speech I ever heard from her.

'How . . .' I began.

'I will walk to the village and someone there will take me to a station.' She seemed so determined. How long had she been making her plans?

'Where will you go?'

'Where the need is greatest.' Her voice was quiet and toneless.

'But you are only fifteen,' I protested.

'I am strong.'

Such confidence left me feeling weak and bewildered. I stepped out of the room and softly closed the door.

Later that morning I heard a muffled sobbing coming from my brother's room. I looked in and found him curled on the floor, his arms covering his face.

'What is it?' I asked, and when his sobs grew more intense, 'Peter, please tell me. Don't shut me out.'

He sat up, then, and told me everything. How Magda had tried so hard to belong. She had never had a real family, only a mother who was forever leaving her with strangers. He told me that as I lay dying my sister's tireless care had saved my life, and her weeks of devotion had almost made a ghost of her. Yet still she had persevered, desperate to earn my friendship and approval. But in the end, my remorseless hatred had beaten her.

'You've driven her away,' sobbed Peter, 'with your stupid, ignorant pride, and she's my sister.'

'Mine too,' I murmured.

'Then stop her, Lena. Only you can do it. She'll stay for you, I know she will.'

I ran from his room, not knowing if I was too late, wrenched open the heavy oak door and stumbled into the icy air. A track of footprints lay in the fresh snow, and I thought I saw a movement by the gate, a fleeting blur against a swirl of silvery white. It had begun to snow again.

'Magda,' I called. 'Sister, please, come back!'

My words were smothered by the falling snowflakes and there was no reply. Soon, even the fragile outline of my sister's feet had vanished.

The Bad Sister

Jacqueline Wilson

It's a beautiful gravestone. A little girl angel spreads her wings, head shyly lowered, neat stone curls never in need of brushing. Her robe is ornately tucked and gathered, a little fancy for an angel frock, as if she's about to attend a heavenly party.

I step over the miniature rosebush and feel along the carving on the gravestone with one finger. I whisper the name.

Angela Robinson.

My name.

Beloved Daughter.

Not me.

Born 1976. Died 1983.

My sister. She died in 1983. I was born in 1984, eleven months later. Another Angela, to replace the first. I suppose that was the theory. Only it hasn't worked out that way. I'm not a little angel.

I reach out and snap the gravestone angel hard on her perky little nose. She smiles serenely back at me, above retaliation. I hit her harder, wanting to push her right off her pedestal. A woman tending a nearby grave looks up, startled. I blush and pretend to be buffing up the angel's cheeks with the palm of my hand.

I haven't been here for a while. Mum used to take me week in, week out, every single Sunday when I was little. I took my Barbie dolls and some scraps of black velvet and played funerals. My prettiest bride Barbie got to be Angela. I sometimes pinned paper-hankie wings on her and made her flap through the air in holy splendour.

One time I dressed her in a nightie and wrapped her up in a plastic carrier bag and started to dig a little hole, all set to bury her. Mum turned round from tidying Angela's flowers and was appalled.

'You can't dig here. This is a cemetery!' she said.

The cemetery seemed a place purpose-built for digging, though I knew enough not to point this out.

Mum was going through a bad patch. Sometimes she seemed normal, like anyone else's Mum, *my* Mum. Then she'd suddenly burst into tears and start a crying spell.

I was always frightened by her tears. There was nothing decorous about her grief. Her eyes were bleary and bloodshot, her face damp and greasy, her mouth almost comically square. I'd try putting my arms round her. She didn't ever push me away but she didn't always gather me up and rock me. Sometimes she scarcely seemed to notice I was there.

She still has crying spells now, even though Angela has been dead for fifteen years. I'll invite Vicky or Sarah home from school and we'll discover Mum crying in the kitchen, head half-hidden in the dishtowel. Birthdays are bad times too. And Christmas is the worst. Angela died in December. A quick dash, an icy road, a car that couldn't brake in time.

One Christmas Mum got so crazy she bought two sets of presents. One pile of parcels for me, one for my dead sister. I don't know how Mum thought she was going to give the first Angela her presents. She could hardly lob them right up to Heaven. I imagined Angela up on her cloud, playing with her big blue teddy and her Little Mermaid doll and her giant rainbow set of felt-tip pens.

After a few weeks my own teddy's plush was matted, I'd given my Little Mermaid doll an unflattering haircut, and I'd pressed too hard on my favourite purple pen so that it wouldn't colour neatly any more. The first Angela's presents stayed pristine.

The first Angela didn't leave the bath tap running so that there was a flood and the kitchen ceiling fell down. The first Angela didn't get into fights at school and poke out her tongue at the teacher. The first Angela didn't bite her nails and tell fibs and wet the bed.

My grandma actually told me to ask Angela for help, as if she'd already acquired saintly status.

'Pray to your sister to help you stop having temper tantrums. Ask Angela for advice on how to stop biting your nails. See if Angela can help you with wetting the bed, your poor mother can't cope with all the extra laundry.'

Dad got furious when he found out, and he and Grandma had a big row. Then Mum and Dad argued too, and for a little while Dad wouldn't let me see Grandma any more. We didn't often see my other gran or any of Dad's family – I think someone had said something tactless about my name way back at my christening and Mum wouldn't speak to them again.

We're still not on really friendly terms with the family – so it was a surprise when the wedding invitation came through the letterbox this morning.

Mum opened it and stared, fingering the deckle-edge.

'What is it?' I asked.

'Nothing,' said Mum. She tried to crumple it up, but it was too stiff.

Dad looked up from his newspaper.

'Is that a wedding invitation?' he said. 'Let's have a look.'

'It's nothing,' Mum repeated, but Dad reached across and snatched it from her.

'Good lord! Becky's getting married,' said Dad.

'My cousin Becky?' I said. 'The one that used to be best friends with Angela?'

Dad usually frowns at me when I mention the first Angela because he doesn't want to set Mum off – but now he just nodded.

'And we're invited to the wedding?' I said. I got up and peered over Dad's shoulder. 'To the ceremony. And the wedding breakfast. Doesn't that sound weird? It's not a real breakfast, is it, like bacon and egg? And a disco in the evening. So . . . are we going?'

'I don't think so,' said Mum.

'I think we ought to go,' said Dad.

'You go if you want. But I don't think I can face it,' said Mum, rubbing her eyebrows with her thumb and forefinger, the way she always does when she has a headache. 'Angela and Becky were just like sisters.'

'So why shouldn't we see Becky married? I've hated

the way we've barely seen the family all these years. I know it's painful, I know it brings back memories – but life goes *on*. It's not fair to me to cut me off from my family. And it's not fair to Angela either.'

'Not fair to *Angela?*' said Mum. It took her a second to realise he meant me.

'I don't *want* to go to Becky's wedding,' I said.

I didn't want all the family looking at me, shaking their heads, whispering. I was sure they'd all compare me with the first Angela. I knew they'd say I wasn't a bit like her.

'There,' said Mum. 'That settles it.' But she looked doubtful.

She picked up her teacup but then put it down without a sip. The cup clattered in the saucer. It was obvious her hand was trembling.

'We'll all go,' Dad said firmly.

'Oh please, don't, both of you,' I said, getting up from the table. 'I'm going to school.'

I rushed off before I could get caught up in the argument. I tried to forget about it. I mucked around with Vicky and Sarah, I got told off for talking in class, I got the giggles in singing, I played the fool on the hockey pitch doing a sword dance with my hockey stick, I wrote a very rude but very funny joke on the toilet wall – while Angela hovered above my head, her wings creating a cold breeze.

I didn't get the bus home with Vicky and Sarah. I walked right through the town and out to the cemetery instead. I don't know why.

Maybe I want to talk to Angela. And yet here I am assaulting her, slapping her stone angel around.

'I'm sorry,' I whisper, and I reach out and hold the angel's hand. Her fist stays clenched. She wouldn't want to hold hands with me. The bad sister.

I'm very late home. Mum is at the window, white-faced. She's already phoned Dad and he's come rushing home from work.

'Where have you *been*?' Mum says, bursting into tears.

'How could you be so thoughtless?' says Dad.

Mum can't ever bear me being ten minutes late because she's so scared there will have been another accident.

'I'm sorry, I'm sorry, I'm *sorry*,' I gabble. 'Look, I went to the cemetery, okay?'

'Oh, darling,' says Mum. She gives me a hug. Even Dad looks sheepish.

I feel guiltier than ever. They think I'm so devoted to my dead sister. They have no idea I sometimes can't stand her.

'Let's have tea,' says Mum.

'What's happening about Becky's wedding?'

'We needn't go. I'll write a note to explain – and we'll send her a nice present,' says Dad.

'Well. Maybe we *should* go. I think I was being a bit . . . selfish,' says Mum. 'We should wish Becky well. Angela – you know, *Angela* – she'd have wanted to go, wouldn't she? And it's right, we have this Angela, *our* Angela, to think of.'

'But I said. I don't want to go.'

It doesn't matter what I say. We're going. And that's that. Dad phones his sister. Mum writes an acceptance note. Dad buys a crystal decanter and glasses as a wedding gift. Mum chooses a new suit, blue with a black trim.

'You'll have to have a suit too, Angela.'

'*Me*?' When I'm out of school uniform I live in jeans and T-shirts.

'Come on now, Angela, use your head,' Mum says impatiently. 'You can't go to a wedding in trousers and trainers.'

She drags me all round this grim department store looking at the most terrible outfits. I moan and complain. Eventually we fetch up in Top Shop and I get a dress and a purple jacket and new shoes. I get quite excited at the way I look. Older, for a start, and although the shoes pinch like hell it's really cool to be wearing sexy high heels.

'You look lovely, Angela,' says Dad, when I dress up for him. I *feel* lovely too.

Not on the wedding day though. My hair won't go right for a start. It sticks out in a terrible frizz and won't be subdued. I've got little spots on my forehead and chin and I slap on so much make-up to cover them it looks like I'm wearing a beige mask. I have to wash and start all over again. I splash water on my dress and I'm scared it will mark. I'm not sure it really goes with the jacket now. My shoes are still beautiful, but whenever I try to walk I turn my ankle.

I'm going to look a right sight at the wedding. I stare at myself in the mirror. The first Angela peeps over my shoulder, her fine eyebrows raised.

Mum's having second thoughts too. When we set off her eyes are red and her nose is shiny and she clutches her lace hankie as if it's a cuddle blanket. Dad puts his arm round her and gives her a quick squeeze.

Everyone stares at us when we get to the church. People hang back as if our stale mourning is contagious – but then my aunt gives my dad a hug and soon everyone's whispering and waving and Mum manages to smile bravely and wave back. I keep my head down, glancing up under my fringe every now and then at all these relations who are practically strangers. I haven't got a clue who half the people are.

There's a good-looking lanky guy with dark hair who peers round at me curiously. He's wearing a shirt the exact royal purple of my jacket. He grins, acknowledging this. I grin back foolishly. And then the organ music starts up and Becky and my uncle start down the aisle.

The dark guy keeps looking at me during the ceremony and the wedding breakfast. (Definitely *not* egg and bacon – and I'm allowed my very first glass of champagne.)

He doesn't come and talk until the disco starts. He stands behind my chair, fingering the jacket I've slung over the back.

'Snap,' he says.

'Snap.'

'Would you like to dance?'

Would I! Though the glass of champagne and my new high heels make me walk very warily onto the dance floor. He is really gorgeous – and he's asked *me* to dance. He's quite a bit older than me too, probably nineteen or twenty. A student. Smiling at me. I hope he doesn't know I'm only fourteen. I don't think he's family.

'What's your name?' I mumble shyly.

'James. And you're Angela.'

'How do you know?'

'Well. I live next door to Becky. I knew your sister.'

I miss a beat.

'You're not a bit like her,' he says.

I knew it.

'Not that I can remember her all that well. I was only a little kid when she ... But I remember that last summer because she came to stay with Becky. She had all this pretty blonde hair and big blue eyes, yes?'

'Like a little angel,' I say. I've stopped dancing.

'Mmm,' says James. He pauses. 'Well. Not exactly *angelic*. I was terrified of her, actually.'

'You were ... what?'

'I was this pathetic little wimp, scared stiff of the big girls. They teased me and I blubbed and that only made them worse.'

'My sister Angela?'

'Becky wasn't too bad, but Angela gave the most terrible Chinese burns. And she had this way of pulling my ears, really twisting them. You're not into ear-twisting, are you?'

I shake my head, still too surprised to joke.

'So Angela really gave you a hard time? I just can't imagine her doing stuff like that.'

'No one else could either. Whenever I told on her she batted those blue eyes and looked so sweet and innocent that no one believed me. I'm sorry. Maybe I shouldn't talk about her like that.'

'No, no – tell me more,' I say, picking up the beat and dancing.

Up above, sparkling in the strobe lighting, Angela is taking off her halo, folding her feathery wings, little horns sprouting through her blonde curls. She's waving her new forked tail at me. My bad sister.

Falling Apples

Anne Fine

It was Antonia who first realised it was to be another of those days. There the four Cox sisters sat, bolt upright in their accustomed places around the polished table. Their pinafores were tugged straight, their hair tied neatly back. Rosie bobbed in and out as usual, with tilting plates and slopping jugs. But as always on these occasions, Mrs Cox barely noticed the tremulous, maladroit serving maid. She only had eyes for her daughters.

'Antonia! Your elbows!'

Not even the frills of her sleeves had brushed the table top, Antonia was sure. But still she made a show of lifting her arms a little. Safer to appease.

'And, Virginia, smirking is deeply unattractive. Do please try to rid yourself of that mean little smile.'

If there were any expression on her sister's face – and that was doubtful – Antonia knew it would have been nothing more than a fleeting look of sympathy. And only someone keeping their mother's unstintingly sharp watch over the four of them would even have noticed it. So she tried to distract with some light remark to Hester about how the rainbow halo cast by the mirror onto the wall above Virginia's head suited that gentlest of sisters perfectly. But Mrs Cox paid no attention. She was, it seemed, working her way around the table as usual.

'Must you *slump* like that, Lucia? You look like a bag of bones. And, Hester, you have a way of stoking food into your mouth that is almost mechanical. Positively *ugly*.'

Ugly, smirking, slumping, clumsy. On and on it would go now, all of them knew, till the last tinkle of the little silver bell, and the merciful release. 'Now, Rosie, you may clear.' On afternoons like these, it was as if a witch had come to tea in Mother's place – a witch whom no one and nothing could please, yet who was clearly sly enough to know how to amuse herself.

For no one else round the table could take any

pleasure in these grim occasions. And any hint of mutiny – the shadows across Virginia's face, Lucia's little pouts, Antonia's short-lived cries of protest, 'But, Mama!' – and the sharp cords of family authority were nipped even tighter.

'Do you dare to contradict me? Are you determined to provoke?'

When they began, these days of wire-taut nerves and thumping hearts, Antonia couldn't recall. And what she and her sisters were afraid of, she couldn't tell, for no one had ever lifted a hand to any of them, she was sure of that. Especially not their father, who steered clear of any unpleasantness. But as far back as Antonia could remember, their mother had had days like these, when every hail-smashed flower stem found in the garden might just as well have been a pit collapse, each message from the kitchen could have been news of a disaster at war, and each laugh from any daughter was a pure affront.

Her fingertips would fly to her temples. 'Girls! Peace! My head is spinning!' But what excuse is that for passing your own misery on like an overhot plate? And finding solace in it. For Antonia had no doubt that, with the witch presiding over the silver teapot, the baiting of each of the sisters round the table in turn served some relieving purpose, as when, through the long winters in the cold, cold house, Antonia herself pressed her sharp fingernails deep in her palms to draw a little of the pain, just for a moment, from her throbbing chilblains.

And no one could deny Mother knew her trade. Safe in the dark of their shared bed, Antonia and Virginia had agreed it was a mystery how easily she could drain the colour from their faces and fill their eyes with tears. As often as not, she'd start with Hester. Not because she was necessarily the easiest of the sisters to unnerve; more because what bit directly into Hester's heart could be approached through easy conversation. It was, after all, the most natural thing to begin with the weather as a topic. From there, to hunting of course. And, after that, seamlessly to animals in general. A short step to pets. And suddenly, tears would be spurting out of Hester's eyes at that apparently so careless reference to dear, dead Hector, most adored of rabbits.

Or, failing that, it would occur to Mrs Cox to ask her girls which way they'd walked that morning. Today, one passing mention of home farm was all it took to do the trick. For how could a girl who had to shut her eyes and be led by her sisters down the path past Jamieson's vegetable plots, even bear open mention of that place where any wheeling gull foolish enough to sail to rest and let itself be trapped, had both wings brutally clipped, and faced a miserable half-life of trawling up and down the furrows, seeking out slugs.

'Such a *shame . . .*' Mother mused, as if the idea had, yet again, occurred to her fresh. 'How those poor creatures must long for sea, and miss the sky!'

And Hester's tears rolled, her own wings equally clipped by the set rule that no one might flee from the table, whatever their distress.

Antonia leaped to her sister's defence. 'Oh, *please*, Mama! Don't let's talk about hateful Mr Jamieson.' But Lucia spoiled her chances of curbing their mother by, in her unthinking and importunate way, going too far. 'Yes, Mother. You absolutely mustn't talk to poor Hester about –'

The target, far from shifting, simply widened.

'Nonsense, Lucia! Hester cannot expect our conversations always to take account of her soft heart. She must learn better self-control. And so must you!'

Ah, this was simplicity itself. For Lucia was 'a brimmer'. To send the fat tears glimmering down her cheeks, all Mother had to do was deepen her frown and remind the poor scrap of all the transgressions born of her precipitous flights around the house and gardens after her precious sister. 'After all, you're no better. Who charged down the pantry passage straight into Maria and broke all those porcelain dishes? Who crashed into my finest rose, and snapped its spine?'

'Do you remember,' Antonia said hastily, 'how it

bloomed even better the next year?'

But it was hopeless. Lucia's eyes still filled. And Mrs Cox moved on around the table.

Me, thought Antonia. Now it's my turn.

But she was wrong. Her mother had already turned to Virginia.

'No news from Stanhope, I take it?'

Virginia flushed scarlet. It was, as everyone around the table knew, the deepest of humiliations for her that, so far, no invitation from the Grange had yet arrived. Everyone else seemed to have been invited to the party – even Drusilla Carter. And if a tradesman's daughter was welcome to spend the afternoon lobbing tennis balls over nets and sipping crushed strawberry ices, then their Virginia must have made a very poor impression on her last visit to the Grange, not to be asked back again.

With no control over the colour of her face, Virginia made an effort to keep her voice unruffled.

'Oh, I do hope the weather holds for them. What could be more dismal than holding a tennis party in the rain?'

'Staying at home, uninvited?' Mother suggested tartly.

Antonia couldn't bear it. 'Perhaps Virginia's only mistake was telling young Stanhope when they were laughing together at the Christmas ball how little she admires the game.'

But it was hopeless. She might as well have tried to shoot a ball back over the net to a champion.

'Virginia is clearly not alone in the business of failing to admire.'

And that was it. Mother had won the match. Up flew Virginia's trembling hands to cover her face, her disappointment and her tears.

And Mother turned to Antonia.

'And what is this I hear from Mrs Fannin about your bruiting your opinions far and wide?'

To give herself a moment to think, Antonia feigned reflection. 'At Sunday School, was that, Mama? Did I mistake something in my lesson for the little ones?'

'I think you understand me well enough, Antonia.'

Antonia steeled herself to gaze, unflinching, into her mother's eyes. Which of her sins would it be? Confessing to Mr Sparrow that she had her doubts about two of the articles in the Holy Creed? Insisting to Miss Hetherington that, on the contrary, blackberries and apples were a very happy mix in pies? Accusing the lads at the ford of horrid cruelty to the frogs they trapped? Or simply offering to Mrs Bethany the housekeeper the opinion that Maria hadn't the strength to carry such heavy coal buckets?

Any. All. None. It made no difference. Clearly, the storm was on its way.

'The apple, of course, never falls far from the tree.

You are fully as outspoken as your father! But what is fitting for a man scarcely befits a silly chit of a girl. What are monkeys and orang-outang and Mr Darwin to do with you? And what embarrassment, to have my own daughter correcting her elders and betters!'

So that was it. A cheerful little wrangle about Creation over a stile with Jamie Crawford's mother! How these petty little reports slunk back.

And how they were used.

'You will, of course, take back your books directly.'

Now this was spite indeed. 'Take back my books?'

'All of them. Every last one. And you must tell Mr Sparrow that he is not to lend you any more.'

'But – '

'No argument, Antonia. How can I let you loose in Mr Sparrow's library if I can't depend on your good sense?'

'But all I said to Mrs Crawford was – '

'Antonia! It's not your place to bicker. No more books!'

Desperately, Antonia looked around for help. Everything else had been horrid, fair enough. But this was *important*. What was she to do without her books? And this was not going to be the sort of rule that was here today and gone tomorrow. Antonia could tell that. This was like being 'too old to paddle in the lake', or, 'forbidden to speak to the Gibsons'. It would stick.

Beside her, little Lucia's hands were wringing in her lap. But of what use was that? Nobody spoke. One by one, Antonia sought their support with pleading eyes. They knew what her books meant. All of their lives, they'd seen her curled up in trees, on window seats, in armchairs, on the bend in the attic stairs, always with a book in her hand. But, one by one, her sisters dropped their gazes safely to the table, leaving her to fight this battle alone.

'But how will I manage? There are so few books here! And Mr Sparrow has so many. He helps me choose, and I know he takes the greatest care not to furnish me with anything he thinks unsuitable. He says so *often*.'

It was like talking to a clear glass wall. Her mother turned away.

'Please, Mother! *Please*!'

'Antonia, be warned. I do dislike scenes at the table.'

A cheap schoolboy trick, to drive a body into a fit of wild misery, then take it to task for its lack of composure.

'This is *not fair*!'

'Each word you utter makes it clear your reading does not so much enrich your young mind as warp it to wilfulness. You'll take every last book straight back to Mr Sparrow within the hour!'

And now the tears of fury and frustration spurted.

Once again, Mrs Cox turned away her face. Was it to hide a look of distaste? Or one of satisfaction? For as this, the last and least fragile of her daughters, finally dissolved into floods, Mrs Cox reached, as if replete at last, for the little silver calling bell.

'Yes, Rosie. Now we're quite finished. You may clear.'

Her heart now as heavy as her bag was light, Antonia strode home through pouring rain, hating her sisters, every last one of them. Despising them utterly. Craven, craven, craven. Hadn't she been the first to spring to poor Hester's defence by begging her mother not to talk any more about horrible Jamieson? Then she'd risked real displeasure by reminding everyone that little Lucia's catastrophe with the rose had led to better things next year. And as for her support of Virginia! Antonia had managed to weave a merry and spirited interchange out of those few stiff words she'd seen exchanged, to no one's satisfaction, at the ball. If she could conjure dignity out of thin air for Virginia, couldn't Virginia speak real truth for her? 'Mother, you know Antonia can't live without her books. Please don't do this to her. *Please* think again.'

And what had they managed between them? Not a word. A few fingers twisting unhappily in a lap, and that was it. But surely sisterhood should work both ways.

And if they were content to make no efforts to keep Antonia herself from bookless misery, why should she strain herself for them? So she might, after all, pass on what Mr Sparrow had let drop about young George Stanhope's opinions. Instead of letting the horrid indiscretion distress only herself, now she could share it. It would, at least, explain the long silence from the Grange, and stop her sister lifting her head in foolish hope each time a letter came. After all, as Mother so often said, the apple never falls far from the tree. Outspoken as her father, Antonia's was a nature on which such a secret might weigh heavily . . . Yes, she would tell.

Over the stile she went, and down the cart-track. And there, snagged in wet brambles, was a spot of pink. It was a ribbon rose from one of Lucia's Sunday frocks. How she'd be panicking! On any other day, Antonia would get herself scratched ragged in the determination to tug it free, and carry it home, triumphant. 'See what I found, Lucia, in the hedge? Now run and fetch thread, and Virginia will make it good before Mother even notices.'

This time, Antonia passed it by without a second look. If the full force of Lucia's efforts to bring things right were simple hand-wringing, then let her wring them for herself. Why should Antonia risk her own dress and her mother's wrath, when no one tried to mend things for her?

Through the swing gate, and into the dripping orchard. And it was fitting that, in this dank place, with her dank heart, she found the baby rabbit, torn by fox or stoat, dead on the footpath where soft, haunted Hester would see it on her way to feed the hens. Antonia drew her foot back just in time. Why kick it into long grass? Let it lie! For that was Hester's way, she'd seen that clearly enough over the table. If you can just do nothing, then just do that.

And here they were, coming across the lawns. Strange, to her, how, with her new resolutions, she felt so much more friendly towards them all and – as if quite forgetting the bloody tangle at her feet – drew them all closer. 'Don't go by the cart-track, Lucia. You will spoil your shoes. Come this way, through the orchard. Virginia, I have such tittle-tattle! You'll never guess what Mrs Sparrow overheard George Stanhope say about you! Do come and hear!'

And even stranger, to them, how, as her voice grew stronger, she herself seemed to be slipping further and further away, back down the wet footpath into the shadow of the largest tree.

A New Dawn

Lynne Markham

'Where are you going?'

'Don't know. Away. Somewhere. Anywhere.'

'But *why*? Is it the Ferret? Is it Bruno? Are you going because of Bruno? Is that it? Or *is* it the Ferret?'

I was talking to Gail, and Gail was chucking things into a bag on her bed: jeans, knickers, a couple of T-shirts, while I stood in front of her, waving my arms about as if that would somehow make her stop. Outside the window you could see Green's Mill glistening under a slick of rain; inside the room Gail was nearly finished, just the sound of my voice made her pause for a second, and look. Then the tight lines round her mouth went soft and she said, 'Listen, Dawn: I'm going because I have to; because of the Ferret; because of Bruno; because of everything. But I'll be back when I'm ready, and I'll write to you, OK? I promise.'

When she said that, Gail picked up her parrot with the stupid red feet and plopped it onto the top of her bag. Then she zipped the bag up and you could still see a bit of the bright red felt sticking out through the metal teeth. Without the parrot her bed looked too empty and bleak, like nobody had ever been in it at all, and I stopped my questions and just stayed quiet. The parrot's going made a kind of full stop; there was nothing else I could think of to say.

Gail was leaving. And it was January.

That was a year ago. And that was when the Ferret really got going. Sneaking up to our room that night and staring at the empty bed. What she did was clasp her hands together over her chest so the cardigan gaped and a button went *ping!* 'Behold!' she said, 'The fury of the Lord shall fall with pain upon the head of the wicked!' Then she looked at the bed again and a smile that wasn't a smile made her lips go thin. 'Jezebel! Her way is the way to hell going down to the chambers of death! The wicked shall be cut off from the earth!'

All this because she thought, or rather she *assumed*, that Gail had gone with Bruno, even though we didn't know for sure, and even though (as we found out later) Bruno was still in Bleasdon, and not with Gail at all. And I just humped back into myself. I didn't even talk to the Ferret or discuss what might have happened. See, I had this idea that the Ferret was happy, that she enjoyed Gail's going off like that; that it satisfied her in some weird way.

Instead of talking I folded my arms and blanked out my eyes and waited deadpan for her to go, which she did, reluctantly, still chuntering on in the way she does: '... my mouth shall speak the truth; wickedness is an abomination on my lips ... the words of my mouth are in righteousness ...'

Then I shut the door and got on the bed and pulled my knees up to my chest and stayed that way for the rest of the night, with my arms clasped tight round my bent-up knees. When morning came I went off to work. I went without speaking a single word, like the house and the Ferret and Gail's going off had somehow made me completely dumb.

Mr Ruben, my boss, says, 'And how are *you* this bright new morning?' He says it every day when he goes past my desk and it's irritating, but kind of nice as well. Because Mr Ruben notices things. He notices, for instance, if you're not very well, even if you've got your make-up on and you answer him back with, 'I'm fine, Mr Ruben, and how are *you*?' in the cheerful voice he expects you to use.

The morning after Gail went away Mr Ruben braked on his heels and came back to my desk and leaned over the switchboard hood and looked into my made-up face.

'Oho!' he said. 'Aunty Etta again! What has she said to my beautiful one? It pains me to think what happened to you! That your parents should go and leave you thus! That she could take two such charming girls and treat them the terrible way she does!'

Mr Ruben always talks as if our parents had gone nonchalantly off into the sunset, deliberately choosing to leave us behind, instead of dying young in a motorway crash.

But Mr Ruben unlocked my tongue. 'Gail's gone,' I said. 'She just packed her bag up yesterday and went off to I-don't-know-where. She said she'll write when she gets herself settled, but without her it's all so – '

Pointless. Blank. So terribly quiet. Why did she go and leave me behind?

'– so strange and quiet. Except for the Ferret who never shuts up.'

'Aha! That woman! You listen, Dawn: you think about Gail. Kind thoughts only! You *will* her back! And maybe tomorrow you'll find her there!'

Mr Ruben believes in mind over matter. He believes that if you want a thing hard enough, if you will it to happen with all your might, then sure enough, one day, it will. He reckons that that's how he got Mrs Ruben; that she was actually going to marry someone else but he applied the force of his own great mind, and she changed hers abruptly and married him instead.

'That's immoral!' I had said to him. And:

'Shuh-shuh! What do you know? Mrs Ruben is happy with me!'

Now I said to him, 'She might have gone somewhere with Bruno. They've seen a lot of each other just lately – most nights at the Club Rascat.'

'Bruno?'

I nodded.

'Bruno with the big arms and hair? No, dear Dawn, Gail would not go with him. Gail is stormy, like her name: she flashes; she dances; she sparkles like rain. This Bruno is dull; he is big, but dull. Definitely Gail would not go with him.'

And Mr Ruben turned out to be right. I saw Bruno in the market square a few days after Gail had gone, leaning against a lamppost looking gloomy, with his hands tucked under his arms for warmth. When I went towards him he just raised his head up off his shoulders and stared at me with his doggy eyes.

'Bruno!' I said. 'Where's Gail? Do you know?'

Bruno shook his head and turned his eyes down again. 'Gail's gone,' he said. He looked hopeless. 'I don't know where. Maybe to London.' He shrugged. Then he sighed and carried on looking at the ground – and that's the thing about Bruno: he's big and good-looking (the girls like him) but he's slow and vague and a bit stupid as well. But Gail went out with him night after night. Gail went out with him to spite the Ferret: 'Evil pursueth sinners, but to the righteous good shall be repaid!'

Gail's feet would go down the hall with the Ferret's voice going after her. Then would come the slamming of the big front door and me alone in the back bedroom. Thinking. Thinking: only three hours till Gail gets back. And wishing I had some friends of my own. Friends that the Ferret couldn't frighten off in the creepy way she always did, so I was stuck on my own in my room all the time with just a battered old radio and a few religious tracts of hers for company.

Thinking: only six months till Gail leaves school; then we can get a flat of our own.

The way it is: Gail's cleverer than me. And more beautiful. Gail stayed on to get her A levels and the flat we'd get when she left school was like a jewel waiting for us. We'd furnish the flat in our imagination and nothing was ever too good for us.

'We'll have check curtains and a wooden floor.'

'Naah,' said Gail, 'I like flowers, me. Chintzy stuff with roses and vines.'

'Laura Ashley with knobs on!' I said.

Then Gail left school and left town as well – and as well as the flat and Aunty Etta, she went off and left me behind, on my own. And Aunty Etta (you have to spit to get the name out right) immediately came into herself.

'He that justifieth the wicked is an abomination!'

Even in bed I could hear her, muttering outside the door. The minute she saw Gail's empty bed she transmogrified right there and then from a ferret snapping at my feet into a full-blown vixen. A vixen red in tooth and claw. And that's when I'd get a hold of my wrists and twist the skin like wringing a cloth. Twist them until they really hurt so the pain of it drove the other pain out: so I wouldn't miss Gail so much any more.

Chinese torture. That's what it was. Gail used to do it to me when we were kids. She'd say: 'See how long it takes till you cry!'

And never a word from Gail for months. Then just a scrappy postcard from Leeds: 'I'm OK, right? Don't worry about me. I'll come back and get you as soon as I can.'

Delivered to me at work.

Mr Ruben saw the card. 'Foolish child!' he said to me. 'You do now what I say before – you *will* dear Gail to come back home.'

That's when I started the mind-bending thing. Not straight away (I thought it was stupid) but later when I was giving up hope. What I did was think about Gail; picture what she might be doing. Picture her getting out of bed; picture her in a coffee bar; picture her dancing in some club. Picture her deciding to come back home.

At first other things got in the way, like I'd slip into thinking about Mum and Dad. I'd brood a bit on the names they gave us (did they know I'd be dark and moody like dawn? And Gail would be so shiny and quick and bright?) – what made them think we'd be so *elemental?* Or at work the phone would ring, and 'Ruben, Ruben, Mayfield and Ruben' would somehow manage to drive Gail away. But after a while I got hooked in.

And that's when a queer sort of change took place. I'd be seeing Gail; picturing her, and knowing that I was, but then something happened without my permission. I started to *act* a lot more like her. I mean brighter. More bolshy: 'Ruben, Ruben, Mayfield and *Ruben*' and cheek the clients the way she would have done. I swear I got taller and put on weight. My hair got lighter and and so did my brain: lighter and quicker. Ideas fizzed and popped in and out of it and Dawn seemed suddenly a long way off; Gail was nearer, she was here and now. And Mr Ruben was doubtful all of a sudden.

'Maybe, Dawn, you relax now, hey? Maybe you have thought enough about Gail, and even now she is on her way home.'

But the truth of it was I *liked* being Gail. Even though I hadn't decided to be her, and it had happened in some sort of freaky way; it was easier, more fun than just being me. I was closer to Gail than when she was home because now there were two of us inside my head. And neither one need ever be lonely.

That's when we went to the Club Rascat. The place I'd never been to before.

Gail and I went there together.

Now I was taller I could wear Gail's clothes: a skirt that was short with shiny bits on it; a T-shirt that ended dead on my waist; lipstick I found in Gail's top drawer.

'Harlot! Thorns and snares are in thy way! Thou liest in wait as for a prey!'

The Vixen swished her tail in the hall, but with Gail's shoes on I could do what I liked: 'At last it shall bite ye like a serpent, and stingeth like an adder!' I said.

After that I marched out of the house and I could picture the Vixen behind me: the fuzzy red hair sticking out from her skull; the narrow face with its dead white skin. And when I got into town I could hear the music jumping along the narrow road. I could hear it before I got to the café, and Gail was saying: 'Go for it! Yeah!' but Dawn was still there, hanging back.

In the end Gail won and we went inside and it was like going into a different world. It was like when we were little and told ourselves stories about what we'd do when we were grown-up, and the stories were a kind of breaking out, so you weren't at home with Aunty Etta, reading the Bible in the cold front room; you were off somewhere dancing; you could be what you liked; you could make things happen if you wanted to.

No one looked at us when we went in. The tables and chairs had been shoved back and the band was playing *Merengue*. No one was even bothering to sit; the band was the beat; the beat was the dance. Merengue Salsa Vallenato.

Dance jumps to the devil's tune!

At the Club Rascat I found out the truth.

Something wrong that was suddenly beautiful. That dance is pure spirit: leaping, turning, letting go. Music tears into you; it cuts you loose and frees you up, so that sometimes what you feel inside is more real than what you actually know.

Like I knew I was Dawn, but I was Gail as well. Gail was the one who lifted her arms and stamped her feet and swayed her body with her eyes tight shut. But Dawn was with her, inside her head, dancing, laughing, flicking her hair; keeping time with her step by step.

Dance leads down to the chambers of hell!

But dance wasn't what the Vixen said. It was different from that, like remembering something you didn't know.

Mr Ruben said, 'What is it, dear Dawn? You look different today. Perhaps you find a young man, hey?'

He was peering over the switchboard again, and his face had this creased-up, imploded look. He looked like an anxious father might – like he wanted me to be happy, right? – but maybe not happy the way I was.

'I went dancing last night, Mr Ruben,' I said. 'It was brilliant! I was dancing all night, near enough.'

'Ah, the dance! That is special. Mrs Ruben and I dance, but – never mind! And did That Woman have anything to say?'

I shrugged. 'She doesn't bother me now. I reckon I'm getting the better of her. It pays if you go and cheek her back.'

'Shuh-shuh, dear Dawn, I understand that, but – there is something I can't quite fathom here – that you should change so much in so short a time. That bothers me, yes, but – never mind! Maybe it's enough you are happy today. Be good, dear Dawn, you hear me now? And maybe soon you hear from Gail.'

But I didn't. Not a word, not a card, not a single line.

Like it wasn't worth her while to stay home for me, so why should she take the trouble to write?

Chinese torture. That's how it was. *Let's see how long before you start to cry.* Except that now there was the Club Rascat.

After that I went every night, near enough, even when the Vixen locked the door. I could get back in through the kitchen window, so I'd be in my bed when she came in to look.

'The spirit of the beast goeth downward to earth.' That's what she said when she saw I was in. But she said it to my humped-up back, and her voice went funny and wobbled a bit, almost as if she could sense what had happened – that I wasn't the usual scaredy-cat Dawn but a different person. Bold, like Gail. Tougher and harder and more alert.

And at the Club Rascat it was different from *that*, Maracas. Drums. The mad guitar. What happened was, they got in my blood, so the cold, grey Dawn disappeared altogether and blossomed into a full-blown Gail.

It was then that I bumped into Bruno again, crossing over the market square. But instead of answering when I spoke to him, he just stared like I was some kind of stranger, and made as if to walk on past

'It's me, you daft thing,' I said to him, rattled, 'me – Gail – as used to be Dawn.'

'Gail's gone,' he said stupidly, staring at me. At my face with Gail's kind of fancy brown make-up, and my hair with its special curly-perm style.

'She's not gone, she's here! I shouted at him. 'Gail's here, I tell you! You're looking at her.'

It was raining and rain ran into my mouth, and Bruno peered at me through the rain.

He shook his head. 'Gail's gone,' he said, 'but she's coming back.' And he put a hand in his donkey jacket and pulled out a piece of scruffy card. Rain made the writing on it run, but Bruno read it out to me, following the words along with his finger:

Coming back. Tell Dawn, will you? But don't go and let the Ferret know.

Love, Gail

Rain like salt was in my mouth. It was dripping off the end of my nose. In front of us the municipal fountain opened and closed like a huge umbrella.

I yelled at Bruno: 'Gail's here, you oaf! She's not coming back! She's standing in front of you already!'

And at the back of my head Mr Ruben spoke: 'I don't know this new person who sits at my desk. I say: where is Dawn? I miss her so much – and Mrs Ruben – she does too. Now I don't talk about Dawn like I did. This new Dawn – she's too pert, too *coming*. She is not so kind as the other Dawn.'

'Well then.' Bruno looked embarrassed. 'Perhaps you should . . . I don't know . . . Stay cool . . .'

He shrugged his shoulders and turned away and began to plod off through the rain.

'Gail's not the person she was, you know!'

I shouted it after him, but he didn't stop, he kept on walking across the square, and the bitter rain fell down like knives.

When I got home I went to my room, and looked in the mirror on top of the chest. The mirror was cloudy, but you could see well enough. The indifferent glass reflected a face, and you could see that the person there wasn't Gail.

It was Dawn. A new Dawn. Staring back.

The way she looked was different from usual; wide-eyed and startled. Not scared, but remembering. Remembering how things used to be.

Thinking: if Gail comes back we'll be separate again. If Gail comes back I'll be on my own.

But then remembering the Club Rascat.

Dance is pure spirit. Leaping. Turning. Finding yourself. With dance you can be what you want to be.

The Girl Jones

Diana Wynne Jones

It was nineteen forty-four. I was nine years old and fairly new to the village. They called me 'The girl Jones'. They called anyone 'The girl this' or 'The boy that' if they wanted to talk about them a lot. Neither of my sisters was ever called 'The girl Jones'. They were never notorious.

On this particular Saturday morning I was waiting in our yard with my sister Ursula because a girl called Jean had promised to come and play. My sister Isobel was also hanging around. She was not exactly with us, but I was the one she came to if anything went wrong and she liked to keep in touch. I had only met Jean at school before. I was thinking that she was going to be pretty fed up to find we were lumbered with two little ones.

When Jean turned up, rather late, she was accompanied by two little sisters, a five-year-old very like herself and a tiny three-year-old called Ellen. Ellen had white hair and a little brown stormy face with an expression on it that said she was going to bite anyone who gave her any trouble. She was alarming. All three girls were dressed in impeccable starched cotton frocks that made me feel rather shabby. I had dressed for the weekend. But then so had they, in a different way.

'Mum says I got to look after them,' Jean told me dismally. 'Can you have them for me for a bit while I do her shopping? Then we can play.'

I looked at stormy Ellen with apprehension. 'I'm not very good at looking after little ones,' I said.

'Oh, go on!' Jean begged me. 'I'll be much quicker without them. I'll be your friend if you do.'

So far, Jean had shown a desire to play, but had never offered friendship. I gave in. Jean departed, merrily swinging her shopping bag.

Almost at once a girl called Eva turned up. She was an official friend. She wore special boots and one of her feet was just a sort of blob. Eva fascinated me, not because of the foot but because she was so proud of it.

She used to recite the list of all her other relatives who had queer feet, ending with, 'And my uncle has only one toe.' She too carried a shopping bag and had a small one in tow, a brother in her case, a wicked five-year-old called Terry. 'Let me dump him on you while I do the shopping,' Eva bargained, 'and then we can play. I won't be long.'

'I don't know about looking after boys,' I protested. But Eva was a friend and I agreed. Terry was left standing beside stormy Ellen, and Eva went away.

A girl I did not know so well, called Sybil, arrived next. She wore a fine blue cotton dress with a white pattern and was hauling along two small sisters, equally finely dressed. 'Have these for me while I do the shopping and I'll be your friend.' She was followed by a rather older girl called Cathy, with a sister, and then a number of girls I only knew by sight. Each of them led a small sister or brother into our yard. News gets round in no time in a village. 'What have you done with your sisters, Jean?' 'Dumped them on the girl Jones.' Some of these later arrivals were quite frank about it.

'I heard you're having children. Have these for me while I go down the Rec.'

'I'm not good at looking after children,' I claimed each time before I gave in. I remember thinking this was rather odd of me. I had been in sole charge of Isobel for years. As soon as Ursula was four, she was in my charge too. I suppose I had by then realised I was being had for a sucker and this was my way of warning all these older sisters. But I believed what I said. I was not good at looking after little ones.

In less than twenty minutes I was standing in the yard surrounded by small children. I never counted, but there were certainly more than ten of them. None of them came above my waist. They were all beautifully dressed because they all came from what were called the 'clean families'. The 'dirty families' were the ones where the boys wore big black boots with metal in the soles and the girls had grubby frocks that were too long for them. These kids had starched creases in their clothes and clean socks and shiny shoes. But they were, all the same, skinny, knowing, village children. They knew their sisters had shamelessly dumped them and they were disposed to riot.

'Stop all that damned *noise*!' bellowed my father. 'Get these children out of here!'

He was always angry. This sounded near to an explosion.

'We're going for a walk,' I told the milling children. 'Come along.' And I said to Isobel, 'Coming?'

She hovered away backwards. 'No.' Isobel had a perfect instinct for this kind of thing. Some of my earliest memories are of Isobel's sturdy brown legs flashing round and round as she rode her tricycle for dear life away from a situation I had got her into. These days, she usually arranged things so that she had no need to run for her life. I was annoyed. I could have done with her help with all these kids. But not that annoyed. Her reaction told me that something interesting was going to happen.

'We're going to have an adventure,' I told the children.

'There's no adventures nowadays,' they told me. They were, as I said, knowing children, and no one, not even me, regarded the War that was at that time going on round us as any kind of adventure. This was a problem to me. I craved adventures, of the sort people had in books, but nothing that had ever happened to me seemed to qualify. No spies made themselves available to be unmasked by me, no gangsters ever had nefarious dealings where I could catch them for the police.

But one did what one could. I led the crowd of them out into the street, feeling a little like the Pied Piper – or no: they were so little and I was so big that I felt really old, twenty at least, and rather like a nursery school teacher. And it seemed to me that since I was landed in this position I might as well do something I wanted to do.

'Where are we going?' they clamoured at me.

'Down Water Lane,' I said. Water Lane, being almost the only unpaved road in the area, fascinated me. It was like lanes in books. If anywhere led to adventure, it would be Water Lane. It was a moist, mild, grey day, not adventurous weather, but I knew from books that the most unlikely conditions sometimes led to great things.

But my charges were not happy about this. 'It's wet there. We'll get all muddy. My mum told me to keep my clothes clean,' they said from all round me.

'You won't get muddy with me,' I told them firmly. 'We're only going as far as the elephants.' There was a man who built life-sized mechanical elephants in a shed in Water Lane. These fascinated everyone. The children gave up objecting at once. Ellen actually put her hand trustingly in mine and we crossed the main road like a great liner escorted by coracles.

Water Lane was indeed muddy. Wetness oozed up from its sandy surface and ran in dozens of streams across it. Mr Hinkston's herd of cows had added their contributions. The children minced and yelled. 'Walk along the very edge,' I commanded them. 'Be adventurous. If we're lucky, we'll get inside the yard and look at the elephants in the sheds.'

Most of them obeyed me except Ursula. But she was my sister and I had charge of her shoes along with the rest of her. Although I was determined from the outset to treat her exactly like the other children, as if this was truly a class from a nursery school, or the Pied Piper leading the children of Hamlin Town, I decided to let her be. Ursula had times when she bit you if you crossed her. Besides, what were shoes? So, to cries of, 'Ooh! Your sister's getting in all the pancakes!' we arrived outside the big black fence where the elephants were, to find it all locked and bolted. As this was a Saturday, the man who made the elephants had gone to make money with them at a fête or a fair somewhere.

There were loud cries of disappointment and derision at this, particularly from Terry, who was a very outspoken child. I looked up at the tall fence – it had barbed wire along the top – and contemplated boosting them all over it for an adventure inside. But there were their clothes to consider, it would be hard work, and it was not really what I had come down Water Lane to do.

'This means we have to go on,' I told them, 'to the really adventurous thing. We are going to the very end of Water Lane to see what's at the end of it.'

'That's ever so far!' one of them whined.

'No, it's not,' I said, not having the least idea. I had never had time to go much beyond the river. 'Or we'll get to the river and then walk along it to see where it goes to.'

'Rivers don't go anywhere,' someone pronounced.

'Yes, they do,' I asserted. 'There's a bubbling fountain somewhere where it runs out of the ground. We're going to find it.' I had been reading books about the source of the Nile, I think.

They liked the idea of the fountain. We went on. The cows had not been on this further part, but it was still wet. I encouraged them to step from sandy strip to sandy island and they liked that. They were all beginning to think of themselves as true adventurers. But Ursula, no doubt wanting to preserve her special status, walked straight through everything and got her shoes all wet and crusty. A number of the children drew my attention to this.

'She's not good like you are,' I said.

We went on in fine style for a good quarter of a mile until we came to the place where the river broke out of the hedge and swilled across the lane in a ford. Here the expedition broke down utterly.

'It's water! I'll get wet! It's all muddy!'

'I'm *tired!*' said someone. Ellen stood by the river and grizzled, reflecting the general mood.

'This is where we can leave the lane and go up along the river,' I said. But this found no favour. The banks would be muddy. We would have to get through the hedge. They would tear their clothes.

I was shocked and disgusted at their lack of spirit. The ford across the road had always struck me as the nearest and most romantic thing to a proper adventure. I loved the way the bright brown water ran so continuously there – in the mysterious way of rivers – in the shallow sandy dip.

'We're going on,' I announced. 'Take your shoes off and walk through in your bare feet.'

This, for some reason, struck them all as highly adventurous. Shoes and socks were carefully removed. The quickest splashed into the water. 'Ooh! Innit *cold!*'

'I'm paddling!' shouted Terry. 'I'm going for a paddle.' His feet, I was interested to see, were perfect. He must have felt rather left out in Eva's family.

I lost control of the expedition in this moment of inattention. Suddenly everyone was going in for a paddle. 'All right,' I said hastily. 'We'll stay here and paddle.'

Ursula, always fiercely loyal in her own way, walked out of the river and sat down to take her shoes off too. The rest splashed and screamed. Terry began throwing water about. Quite a number of them squatted down at the edge of the water and scooped up muddy sand. Brown stains began climbing up crisp cotton frocks, the seats of beautifully ironed shorts quickly acquired a black splotch. Even before this was pointed out to me, I saw this would not do. These were the 'clean children'. I made all the little girls come out of the water and spent some time trying to get the edges of their frocks tucked upwards into their knickers. 'The boys can take their trousers off,' I announced.

But this did no good. The frocks just came tumbling down again and the boys' little white pants were no longer really white. No one paid any attention to my suggestion that it was time to go home now. The urge to paddle was upon them all.

'All right,' I said, yielding to the inevitable. 'Then you all have to take all your clothes off.'

This caused a startled pause. 'That ain't right,' someone said uncertainly.

'Yes it is,' I told them, somewhat pompously. 'There is nothing whatsoever wrong with the sight of the naked human body.' I had read that somewhere and found it quite convincing. 'Besides,' I added, more pragmatically, 'you'll all get into trouble if you come home with dirty clothes.'

That all but convinced them. The thought of what their mums would say was a powerful aid to nudity. 'But won't we catch cold?' someone asked.

'Cavemen never wore clothes and they never caught cold,' I informed them. 'Besides, it's quite warm now.' A mild and misty sunlight suddenly arrived and helped my cause. The brown river was flecked with sun and looked truly inviting. Without a word, everybody began undressing, even Ellen, who was quite good at it, considering how young she was. Back to nursery teacher mode again, I made folded piles of every person's clothing, shoes underneath, and put them in a long row along the bank under the hedge. True to my earlier resolve, I made no exception for Ursula's clothes, although her dress was an awful one my mother had made out of old curtains, and thoroughly wet anyway.

There was a happy scramble into the water, mostly to the slightly deeper end by the hedge. Terry was throwing water instantly. But then there was another pause.

'*You* undress too.' They were all saying it.

'I'm too big,' I said.

'You *said* that didn't matter,' Ursula pointed out. 'You undress too, or it isn't *fair*.'

'Yeah,' the rest chorused. 'It ain't *fair!*'

I prided myself on my fairness, and on my rational, intellectual approach to life, but . . .

'Or we'll all get dressed again,' added Ursula.

The thought of all that trouble wasted was too much. 'All right,' I said. I went over to the hedge and took off my battered grey shorts and my old, pulled jersey and put them in a heap at the end of the row. I knew as I did so, why the rest had been so doubtful. I had never been naked out of doors before. In those days, nobody ever was. I felt shamed and rather wicked. And I was so big, compared with the others. The fact that we all now had no clothes on seemed to make my size much more obvious. I felt like one of the man's mechanical elephants, and sinful with it. But I told myself sternly that we were having a rational adventurous experience and joined the rest in the river.

The water was cold, but not too cold, and the sun was just strong enough. Just.

Ellen, for some reason, would not join the others over by the hedge. She sat on the other side of the road, on the opposite bank of the river where it sloped up to the road again, and diligently scraped river-mud up into a long mountain between her legs. When the mountain was made, she smacked it heavily. It sounded like a wet child being hit.

She made me nervous. I decided to keep an eye on her and sat facing her, squatting in the water, scooping up piles of mud to form islands. From there, I could look across the road and make sure Terry did not get too wild. They were, I thought, somewhat artificially, a most romantic and angelic sight, a picture an artist might paint if he wanted to depict young angels (except Terry was not being angelic and I told him to *stop throwing mud*).

They were all tubular and white and in energetic attitudes, and the only one not quite right for the picture was Ursula with her chalk-white skin and wild black hair. The others all had smooth fair heads, ranging from near white in the young ones, through straw yellow, to honey in the older ones. My own hair had gone beyond the honey, since I was so much older, into dull brown.

Here I noticed how *big* I was again. My torso was thick, more like a petrol drum than a tube, and my legs looked *fat* beside their skinny little limbs. I began to feel sinful again. I had to force myself to attend to the islands I was making. I gave them landscapes and invented people for them.

'What you doing?' asked Ellen.

'Making islands.' I was feeling back-to-nature and at ease again.

'Stupid,' she said.

More or less as she spoke, a tractor came up the lane behind her, going towards the village. The man driving it stopped it just in front of the water and stared. He had one of those oval narrow faces that always went with people who went to Chapel in the village. I know I thought he was Chapel. He was the sort of age you might expect someone to be who was a father of small children. He looked as if he had children. And he was deeply and utterly shocked. He looked at the brawling, naked little ones, he looked at Ellen, and he looked at me. Then he leant down and said, quite mildly, 'You didn't ought to do that.'

'Their clothes were getting wet, you see,' I said.

He just gave me another, mild, shocked look and started the tractor and went through the river, making it all muddy. I never, ever saw him again.

'Told you so,' said Ellen.

That was the end of the adventure. I felt deeply sinful. The little ones were suddenly not having fun any more. Without making much fuss about it, we all quietly got our clothes and got dressed again. We retraced our steps to the village. It was just about lunch time anyway.

As I said, word gets round in a village with amazing speed. 'You know the girl Jones? She took thirty kids down Water Lane and encouraged them to do wrong there. They was all there, naked as the day they was born, sitting in the river there, and her along with them, as bold as brass. A big girl like the girl Jones did ought to know better! Whatever next!'

My parents interrogated me about it the next day. Isobel was there, backwards hovering, wanting to check that her instinct had been right, I think, and fearful of the outcome. She looked relieved when the questions were mild and puzzled. I think my mother did not believe I had done anything so bizarre.

'There is nothing shameful about the naked human body,' I reiterated.

Since my mother had given me the book that said so, there was very little she could reply. She turned to Ursula. But Ursula was stoically and fiercely loyal. She said nothing at all.

The only result of this adventure was that nobody ever suggested I should look after any children except my own sisters (who were strange anyway). Jean kept her promise to be my friend. The next year, when the Americans came to England, Jean and I spent many happy hours sitting on the church wall watching young GIs stagger out of the pub to be sick. But Jean never brought her sisters with her. I think her mother had forbidden it.

When I look back, I rather admire my nine-year-old self. I had been handed the baby several times over that morning. I took the most harmless possible way to disqualify myself as a child-minder. Nobody got hurt. Everyone had fun. And I never had to do it again.

Family Portrait

Maeve Henry

To know what happened, you have to understand that
Vanessa, my sister, has always wanted to be normal. I
don't mean she's disabled or mad or anything. I just
mean she has always wanted to be like anyone else.

We were close when we were little. The summer
when I was six – Van must have been eight – we used to
hide, giggling, on family picnics, and time how long it
took the grown-ups to notice we were missing. I think it
was the next summer we decided to build our own
volcano in the back garden. I can remember hours of
muddy digging, and Vanessa's mad excitement when the

hot red soap suds came squirting up out of the hidden tube. Then Vanessa started at a new secondary school, and suddenly I was her bratty little sister. The things she used to like were an embarrassment. I can remember we had a huge row when she wanted to take down the Chagal postcards on the wall of the bedroom we shared, and put up a poster of some awful boy band.

'But you don't even like them!' I wailed in protest. 'You never listen to pop.'

'I do now,' Vanessa said. 'Everyone does.'

'You're not everyone. You're different, Van.'

Vanessa shrugged. 'You'll learn, Carrie,' she said. She was trying to look sophisticated, but underneath I thought she was miserable. She talked about her friends a lot, but she never brought them home. It was only when I started at that school myself that I got to know them. Patsy Scott cornered me in the dining hall almost on the first day.

'Van says your dad is too lazy to get a proper job, and that's why you two look like Oxfam rejects.'

I stared over her shoulder at Van, who met my outraged stare with a look that was half pleading, half mutinous.

'It's true,' she said to me. 'He could work if he wanted.'

'What he does *is* work,' I pushed past them both

angrily. 'He just doesn't get paid for it, that's all.'

I told Vanessa she should find new friends, and she retorted she was perfectly happy with the ones she had, thanks. Now the distance was growing on both sides. At school I avoided her as much as possible, and at home, if she talked about Patsy and Khalida, we ended up rowing. I had my own friends by then, and I suppose I let them fill the gap. My best friend Rachel started staying over at our house on Saturdays. She loved the way Mum came downstairs from her studio in her work clothes at about eight, and poked about in the fridge as if hoping someone had left a roast chicken in it. Dad usually came home a bit later from the studio he rents, and eventually Mum would throw some tins together and cook up pasta or rice and we would have what passed for supper. Rachel and I wheedled beer out of Dad and teased him about still smoking. It was how things used to be with Vanessa and me. I stopped caring that Vanessa sat by herself, flicking aimlessly through magazines, not talking. Sometimes she even put her Walkman on to blot us all out.

'I'll cook a curry for you soon, Van,' Dad would promise with his most charming smile, but Vanessa only scowled. Nothing about us pleased her any more.

Rachel thought it was wonderful to live as we did.

But Rachel didn't see the other side of it. On Monday mornings her school uniform would be ready, newly washed and ironed. I never caught her scrabbling through the laundry basket for a pair of tights to wear, nor trekking to the phone box because her dad forgot to pay the phone bill. I shared Vanessa's frustration, or I thought I did. I thought I knew her. I thought that, sooner or later, Vanessa would give us all that big grin of hers, shrug her shoulders, and admit that she'd been silly. I didn't know how far away she had already gone from us in her head, how far she was prepared to go.

So this is how it happened, how we were all blown apart. It started in a very ordinary way. Mum has a cousin called Alex, and he wrote to say he was moving out of London to Oxford. Not to the slummy bit where we live, but to North Oxford where the houses are huge, with smart cars in the drive. Mum isn't very close to her own family, but she was quite keen to see Alex again and to catch up with his children, Dominic and Louise, who are around our age. So we phoned them, and invited them for a meal. Dad even promised to cook, though he muttered darkly about them being snobs and philistines.

The evening, when it came, was a disaster. Alex wore an amused and patronising smile the whole time. He asked how much money Mum's work currently fetched, and whether Dad's long overdue exhibition would ever take place. He made jokes about our house being an installation and about finding pickled animals in the curry. Louise simply looked bored. Patsy made an effort with Mum, trying first domestic chit-chat, then current affairs. But the vague or irrelevant answers she got drove her back into puzzled silence. I knew Mum didn't mean to be rude; she was worrying about whether she'd cooked enough rice, and whether the loo would flush properly when the visitors used it. Patsy asked for the bathroom, and when she came down again, I could tell from her tight expression that it hadn't.

I haven't, you may have noticed, said anything about Dominic. This is because it was obvious to everyone that something was happening between Vanessa and him.

They were sitting together on the bench at one end of the table, and almost as soon as they sat down, they began talking together in low voices. Dominic, at seventeen, is almost miraculously spot free, fair-haired and handsome.

'Isn't he a bit dim, though?' I whispered to Vanessa while we were rummaging in the cupboard for enough coffee cups for all of us. 'He doesn't know who the Minister for Arts is, and he thinks pointillism is a computer game.'

Vanessa reddened. 'Just because you go for

undersized dwarfs who play the piano,' she retorted. 'Khalida and I had good laugh about that.'

I had told her about David Ginsburg in strictest confidence, so that really made me angry.

'Mum and Dad won't like it if you start going out with him.'

Vanessa raised her chin stubbornly. 'They wouldn't notice I was going out with anyone till I presented them with a grandchild,' she retorted. 'It's none of their business and you know it.'

As soon as the cousins had left, Dad poured himself some more wine and began mimicking Alex's manner, and mocking Dominic's clothes and opinions. Mum and I giggled, but Vanessa didn't. She stood very still, staring at the greasy water in the sink. Then she raised her voice and stared at Dad.

'I don't see what's so stupid about Next and Gap,' she said. 'I don't see what's so funny about Dominic wanting to do business studies. I think it's great to be able to take your family on holiday to France, and buy them cellos and computers. You think you've made up for it because you've told us who Kandinsky was. But I don't care about art! I care about – about having the things they have.'

Mum and Dad looked at her, appalled.

'I'm going to bed,' Vanessa said.

'Me too,' I said quickly, but Vanessa wouldn't talk to me, not even when we were lying across the room from each other in the dark.

I knew she was seeing Dominic, but she never spoke to me about it. I think Mum guessed. She started asking Van where she was going if she went out, something my parents never bothered with before.

'Khalida's,' Van would reply tersely. But the night I phoned her from Rachel's, she wasn't there.

One Saturday night a few months later, I came home from a party. I had planned to stay at a friend's, but she drank too much and was sick and her mother drove her home early.

As soon as I opened our front door, I heard the voices. Dad sounded more puzzled than angry.

'I just don't see why it has to be him. He's so – so ordinary.'

'Normal, you mean?' Vanessa's voice was strained and sarcastic.

'I just think you could find someone more interesting, someone more like you,' Mum was saying warmly. 'There'll be plenty of time to look around when you get to college.'

'College?' Vanessa started to shout. 'You really think

I'm going to go to college? How, Mum? There are fees now, you know, and the grants aren't worth tuppence. Khalida's dad's taken out some sort of savings plan already, but you two –'

Dad, for the first time, sounded genuinely shocked. 'I'm sure with your brain –' he began.

'You don't know anything about my brain,' Vanessa interrupted. 'You've never even read my school reports.' Now she was really crying. 'The only person who knows anything about me is Dominic.'

I went into the kitchen then, but no one took any notice of me.

'That's not true, Van.'

Mum tried to take her hand, but Vanessa wouldn't let her. 'I know it hasn't always been easy for you two, but we've tried our best.'

Vanessa shook her head, wiping her eyes on the back of her hand. 'No you haven't. You've tried your best to paint, and we've been an afterthought.'

'Van!' Mum was really distressed now. She turned to Dad with a look of desperate appeal. He tried to smile and said lightly, 'Come on now, Van, what did you expect us to do? Get jobs and be Sunday painters all our lives?'

Vanessa only looked at him. For a moment Dad seemed completely unnerved, but then anger took over.

'Well if that's the case, if money is all you care about,

then you and Dominic deserve each other!' he shouted. 'But I never thought my own daughter would turn out to be so – so mediocre!'

He was too upset to see the look of pure hate that flared in Vanessa's face. I saw it, and I was scared.

'OK, Dad,' Vanessa said quietly. 'If that's how you want it.'

She went out of the room, and I followed her quickly. She was lying on her bed in the dark. I went over and sat on the edge of the bed. I could hear her crying.

'Do you love him?' I asked.

'He loves me,' she said. 'He does, Carrie. When I'm sixteen, he wants me to go and live with him.'

I was astonished. 'What about his parents?'

'They don't mind. They're really sweet. And their house – you should see it! I'd have my own room. And I'd go to the same school as Dom.'

'Sounds like you've got it all planned out,' I said wryly. 'Is that what the row was about?'

'God, no. Dad had finally noticed I was seeing Dominic, that's all.' She sat up suddenly and her voice became fierce. 'I won't forgive him for what he said. I'll find some way to hurt him like he hurt me. I will, Carrie.'

Vanessa didn't talk to me again about Dominic after that night. She didn't talk to me about anything much, and when Mum and Dad were around, she retreated into wounded silence. I wanted Mum to speak to Van, but she said it was better just to leave it. Dad seemed to have completely forgotten about it in the excitement of getting his long awaited exhibition organised at last. He was going to show his work at a small gallery in London and he was hoping for some reviews and plenty of sales.

'We'll blow it all on a trip to Italy,' he promised. 'I'll take you to Florence.' He turned to Mum with one of his charming smiles. 'How long ago did we go together?'

'We must have been twenty.' Mum closed her eyes for a moment, remembering.

Vanessa shrugged. 'I'm looking for a holiday job,' she said shortly. 'I expect you'll manage without me.'

There were a lot of canvasses to get ready. In the run up to the exhibition Dad kept most of them in the studio upstairs. The most striking was a portrait of Mum in oils. I liked it very much. It showed her framed in our kitchen doorway, dressed in her painting clothes. Her hair was tumbling down her back and she was laughing. Dad had spent months on it. There was a quality about it that I can't describe; I thought it was the best thing he had ever done. Dad must have thought so too, for when he showed us the catalogue for the exhibition, that picture was described as 'Not for Sale'.

'He's too fond of it to let it go,' Mum told me, with a

look of deep happiness. 'But it's the centre of this collection.'

Dad had hired a van to take the paintings into London himself. It was the first Saturday of the summer holidays, and I had persuaded him to let me go too. We were happy as we began to load up the paintings. Dad had promised to take me somewhere special for lunch, and was teasing me with names of the dishes – pani puri, masale dosa – and making me try to guess what was in them. Then he noticed that the protective wrapping round Mum's picture was torn across and the picture itself was showing through. He leant it carefully against the front door.

'Wait here,' he said. 'I'll just fetch some tape to fix that.' He went back into the house and ran upstairs.

I stood on the pavement watching the open door of the van. Then I heard our phone ring, and Dad pick it up. At that moment, our neighbour, Mrs Kelsey, wandered out to see what was happening. She's a kind old thing, so I let her have a good peer at the inside of the van, and a look at the catalogue. Perhaps I spent five minutes with her. I can't see her now without a sick feeling in my stomach. She said goodbye, and I heard Dad running down the stairs. Then he made this awful noise, something between a scream and a sob. I turned and saw what had happened. The picture was lying on the ground, its wrapping torn off, the canvas torn and hacked. Mutilated. Dad looked at me, white and sick. He couldn't speak. Neither could I. I knew at once, you see.

I found the knife eventually, hidden under her mattress, still with flakes of red and blue paint on its blade. When Dad spoke of it later he blamed vandals. And me, for not watching. He acted like someone who had been mugged. His confidence in himself was shaken, and it never properly came back. That was what Vanessa wanted, of course. In September, after her birthday, she went to live with Dominic. She seems very happy in that big warm house. I go to see her sometimes. We look like sisters, but we're not the same inside any more. I should have seen it coming.

I should have been able to stop it happening. That's what I keep thinking. Perhaps Van thinks that too. For the moment all I can do is keep her secret. But I mean to get her to talk to me about it. Even if I have to wait until we are old, I'll do it. She can't keep me out all her life.

Half Term Sister

Joanna Carey

'It's just a small operation,' said Mum briskly. 'Routine really, no need to go into details, nothing to make a fuss about.'

Just get it over and done with. Just like when Dad left. Self-contained, my mum. Me too, I suppose.

She'd be in hospital over the autumn half-term.

'You can stay with us, Daveen,' said Sadie and Sue next door. 'We're going to Gran's – in the country – and she said to bring a friend. Say you will, Davey. Please! It's boring there when it's just us!'

I wasn't sure about this; I'd known Sadie and Sue for

ever – but as neighbours rather than close friends. Compared with me and my mum in our tidy first floor flat, their domestic arrangements were all over the place – practically no rules or regulations – and they never stopped teasing me about my orderly existence, my homework and my sensible clothes.

But we had a sort of understanding. They were cool and daring in a way I'd never want to be, and at school, just being around them gave me a kind of street cred that left me free to be myself.

They thought it was 'really weird' that I'd never spent a night away from home and they kept on at me about half-term. I wasn't keen, neither was Mum . . . 'But you'll have to go somewhere,' she said. 'At least you'd be out of London there. I'm sure those two are up to no good, but the parents are nice enough and I daresay their gran's got her head screwed on. And it's the nearest you'll ever get to having sisters of your own, so you may as well make the most of it.'

Funny how she ignores the fact that Dad's got a new baby daughter. Chantal, she's called – but Mum's pulled the shutters down on the subject of Dad, and she expects me to do the same. It's difficult though. I've been brought up to feel good about being an only child – 'special', my mum's always said – and it's unsettling to find out all of a sudden that I've got a half-sister.

Nobody's ever thought to ask me how I feel – not just about *having* a sister, but about *being* one – or half one, anyway. I'd give anything to see Chantal but it's out of the question. Mum'd hit the roof – or she'd break down in tears. I can't stand that sort of thing. So I end up treating her like an unexploded bomb – everyone feels guilty and nothing gets said. Dad keeps well out of it.

So off I went with Sadie and Sue to Sussex. Their gran's cottage, next to the vicarage, was in a lovely little village – all cosy, neat and tidy like in the Miss Marple films. Gran – she said to call her that – was tall and dramatic-looking, not that old. She had a dark, chocolatey voice and white hair that had gone all yellow at the front from smoking. She wore loads of clunky jewellery and made dramatic gestures, a bit actressy. Showy, my mum would have said. I wasn't sure I liked her. 'Daveen?' she said when Sadie and Sue introduced me. 'That's a curious name!'

'My dad invented it,' I mumbled. 'He's called David and my mum's Eileen – silly isn't it?'

Gran laughed, 'Oh, I don't know! Could have been worse. You could have been called Eyelid!' Sadie and Sue fell about laughing. I blushed right down to my elbows.

My heart sank further when I heard about the harvest festival celebrations. The village church was already stacked up with piles of vegetables – a bit like the organic shelves in Tesco's – and Gran was organizing a fancy dress contest for teenage girls, in order to select a harvest queen (an old custom, she said, that Milton refers to in *Paradise Lost*). And *we* were supposed to dress up and take part. That's why I'd been invited. I felt really cheesed off. What a hideous, phoney business. Harvest queen! I mean, what do they take me for? And talk about sexist! – 'Cattle Market,' my mum would have said. I'd just as soon enter a Miss World contest. 'I'm having nothing to do with this,' I said.

'Typical!' said Sadie.

'Spoilsport,' said Sue (she always echoes Sadie). 'Relax, Dave! If only for Gran's sake! It'll be a laugh.'

But it was a nightmare. For a start I had to share a room with Sue and Sadie. I'd never been all that chummy with them – or anyone, come to that. OK, we used to play together when we were little – Barbie dolls, hospitals and pretend tea parties – but that certainly didn't involve the appalling enforced intimacy of being 'sisters' for a whole weekend. This was something else. This was a Barbie slumber party from hell.

Sadie and Sue were real 'touchy-feely' types, forever pushing, kissing, nudging, slapping, hugging each other. And they had a private way of silently staring round-eyed at one another, each knowing exactly what the other was thinking. It was unnerving. I envied their closeness just as I was repelled by it. They'd wander round our room stark naked as if it was completely normal. They'd quarrel like wild cats over daft bits of jewellery and make-up – and the next minute they'd be painting each others' toenails or swapping nose-rings. They'd chat away while one of them was in the bath, the other on the loo. I didn't get a moment's privacy even when I got undressed – 'God you're skinny!' they squealed. 'You're so lucky, Dave!' And they asked incredibly personal questions about me and Mum. What exactly was this operation she was having? How old was she? And my dad – was it true he'd run off with a French woman? Talk about intrusive! I was horrified by their relentless questioning, and by the details they somehow extracted from me; things my mum would have said were 'nobody's business but your own.' I felt such a traitor telling them about Chantal. They were amazed and went all gooey at the thought of me having a little sister. But they were shocked when I said I'd never seen her. Not even a photo.

Sadie tactfully changed the subject but there was no way I was going to sit up all night discussing costumes for this tacky fancy dress parade. Left to myself, I suppose, although I wouldn't have wanted to dress up, I'd have been in the library researching classical figures like Demeter, Persephone, Dionysus. I might have found inspiration in a pre-Raphaelite painting, or a poem, but with these airheads I had to distance myself from the whole thing.

Difficult though, because Gran was busy clearing her attic. She emptied onto our bedroom floor three bin-bags full of old clothes for us to dress up in.

'The things I used to wear in the fifties and sixties!' she shrieked. 'Honestly! I can't believe it!'

Neither could I. Strapless ball-gowns, cartwheel hats, feather boas, fake furs, Afghan waistcoats, thigh high boots and tarty stiletto heeled slingbacks. And the underwear! Boned corsets, rubbery beige suspender belts and even an ancient pair of school bloomers with elasticated legs. 'What we used to call "harvest festival knickers," said Gran – you know, *'all is safely gathered in'*!'

Sadie and Sue screeched with laughter and Gran cackled like a witch. There's a very vulgar streak in that family. Gran saw me looking at her. She took my hand, suddenly all serious.

'Clothes can tell you such a lot about a person. Some of us, like me I suppose, want to attract attention while others just want camouflage. Clothes are a disguise, but deep down we're all pretty much the same. "Sisters under the skin." Now, who was it who said that?'

'Kipling,' I answered, getting a savage 'know-all' look from Sadie.

'Anyway, girls, don't let me down tomorrow! Interpret the harvest theme however you want. Express yourselves! Outrageous as you like. Anything you don't want, sling it back in the bag. I'm sure poor Marjorie will be glad of it.' ('Poor Marjorie' lived over the village shop with her mum. She was 16. Abandoned by her bloke, she already had twin daughters aged one and was expecting another baby any minute.)

Tentatively, Sadie and Sue picked out a few choice items – including a shimmering gold shawl that Gran said she'd worn at her wedding (she married at 17, imagine!) and a beautiful velvet cape that really did have the dusky bloom of freshly picked plums. But soon they were strutting about in baby doll pyjamas, vinyl boots and silly hats. I had a bit of a laugh, and actually there were some Grecian sandals I fancied but Gran's feet were size 8. And besides, I wasn't going to start tarting myself up.

'You're pathetic, Dave,' said Sadie, 'it's just a bit of fun.'

'That's right,' said Gran. 'Come on, Daveen! So what if it's a bit over the top! Remember, with 2000 years of history behind it, this village has seen things a lot more alarming than a raunchy fancy dress parade. I'm sure we can accommodate a new slant on pagan high spirits!'

'But won't your vicar be expecting you . . . and us . . . to take this . . . well . . . a bit more seriously?' I said, (sounding like my mum, I know).

'Oh, chill out, Dave!' said Sadie, squeezing into a hideous psychedelic jump suit. 'For God's sake, it's not as if we're nuns.'

Woken next morning by the sound of church bells mingled with the pulsating thud of a drum'n'bass track, we leapt to the bedroom window. Sound system blaring, a battered old transit van was parked in the vicarage drive. The vicar's niece, also invited to swell the numbers, had arrived with a crowd of student friends. We saw Gran handing out coffee and showing the girls where to get changed.

Sensing a challenge – and totally abandoning any thoughts of an artistic interpretation of the 'harvest' theme, Sadie hurriedly pulled on hot pants, a see-through crocheted top that showed off her tattoo, and long mushroom suede boots. Sue chose fishnet tights, a ruched nylon swimsuit, elbow length gloves and the velvet cape I'd secretly had my eye on.

'I'm staying here,' I said, but Sue grabbed me. 'You can't not dress up. Please! Sadie'll be livid,' she said in an urgent whisper, shovelling me into Gran's old leopard-print maxi coat. It was miles too big, shabby and it stank of stale perfume but actually it was perfect – I could hide in it. Just to show willing, I put some apples in a little old basket. 'Mellow Fruitfulness,' I said to nobody in particular, 'and that's Keats if anyone wants to know.' Nobody did.

We squelched across the field in the autumn mist to the corner of the churchyard where Gran was lining up contestants. With costumes celebrating so many aspects of nature's abundance, it was a bizarre gathering. One girl had come on a bike; festooned with ivy, its basket was full of windfalls and a dead pheasant hung from the handlebars; shot I suppose, though secretly I hoped it had only been run over. Another girl had stitched hundreds of autumn leaves on to a leotard, and carried a home-made loaf. Alongside them, Sadie and Sue, all glitter and cleavage with loads of blusher and fruity lipstick, looked like larky Blind Date contestants who'd strayed on to the set of Blue Peter. I snuggled up in my leopardskin 'fun fur' and tried to vanish in the mist.

Then, bulging out of one of Gran's hippie kaftans, Poor Marjorie arrived, bumping her double buggy over the field. We all shoved up to make room. You couldn't help smiling at her fat babies. Side by side, in orange Babygros, they looked like a pair of prize pumpkins. For a moment I thought of Chantal – surely she wouldn't be as podgy as that?

As the mist turned to drizzle, I watched Sadie and Sue sizing up the competition. I expected a subversive wink, but realized with a shock how seriously they were taking all this nonsense as we waited for the vicar and the judges.

At the last moment yet another figure came bounding across the field from the vicarage. Elegant in Grecian sandals, skilfully dodging the cowpats, this last minute contender for the harvest crown wore a floaty muslin shift, loosely draped and tied at the waist with a length of binder twine. A garland of wild flowers was looped over floppy curtains of corn-coloured hair that almost obscured cheekbones *to die for*. Everyone gawped as the latecomer skidded to a halt, took a deep breath and solemnly assumed a carefully rehearsed classic pose. What style! What grace! With a beatific gaze fixed on a distant horizon, here was a *real* corn goddess. Your actual Demeter!

I thanked my lucky stars I hadn't attempted anything like that. A press photographer pushed forward. The judges were transfixed. There were mutters of discontent from the crowd – 'Obviously a model,' said one woman. 'So tall! Such poise! It's not fair! This should be for our local girls!'

Sadie and Sue looked on venomously, wishing they hadn't played it for laughs. I felt for them, I really didn't want to see them ridiculed.

It was about to rain. The judges conferred and just as the vicar announced the winner the church bells began to ring out. No one could hear him but it was no surprise to see him place the crown on the modestly inclined head of the lovely Demeter.

But suddenly, shouting inaudibly at the vicar against the violent jangling of the bells, the lovely Demeter removed the crown, kicked off the sandals and took off at a cracking pace across the field. Hoiking up the flimsy dress to reveal brawny thighs and tartan boxer shorts, he vaulted effortlessly over the gate and into the waiting transit van which zoomed off with all the students laughing their heads off.

Gran merely shrugged dismissively and picked up the crown. She handed it back to the startled vicar who, in a state of shock, gently placed it on Poor Marjorie's head. Marjorie beamed, gave him a hug and burst into tears. Then the rain started. The bells rang out, the heavens opened.

The village girls all ran for the church porch but I slipped off the maxi coat and held it up as a shelter. Gran joined me, then Sadie and Sue. Make-up all streaky with rain and humiliation, they looked completely wrecked. Should I laugh or what? They stared silently at one another – usually their way of shutting me out, but Sue caught my eye and suddenly I was tuned in. We stared into each others' thoughts for almost a full half-minute. Then Sue sneezed and one of her (very '60s) false eyelashes peeled off and started inching down her face like a caterpillar. Gross! Sadie gave a long shuddering sob of laughter . . . and pushing, shoving, sobbing, hugging we all collapsed in a comfortable heap of giggles in the mud.

Above us the rain gathered in a puddle on the coat and slowly began to plop through. Gran nudged me and, with a scarlet fingernail, jabbed at the acrylic fur.

'See?' she said. 'We're all in this together – sisters under the skin! . . . that's Kipling, you know.'

Back at the cottage, reliving the coronation – and the abdication – of the harvest queen we nearly died of laughter. 'Pity we never got hold of him,' said Sadie – she'd quickly recovered her self-esteem – 'I'd have enjoyed having a go at de-frocking him . . .'

Later on though, sitting by the fire with Gran, I was furious when I realized the girls had been blabbing out all my secrets.

'Not blabbing, Daveen! Talking. Like friends *do*,' said Gran sharply. 'Now tell me, how was your mum when you phoned her? You must be dying to get back to her. Away from this madhouse! And you must be excited about your dad's new baby! How's your mum taken it? Difficult for her I imagine. And what about you – how does it feel to be the big sister? I bet you're longing to get involved. Do you see much of your dad?'

It was a shock to hear these things said out loud. To talk like that at home would have been like flinging hand grenades through the net curtains of our living room. But without the background of tears, guilt, embarrassment and disapproval that I was used to, Gran's questions were straightforward and perfectly reasonable. It was like a fog had lifted. I could see where I was going; I was going straight home to have a good long talk with my mum. Get things sorted. There's no point pretending Chantal doesn't exist, but she's only a baby! – it's not as if she's a missile on course to destroy Mum's relationship with me, or to invade our territory. (And yes, Gran was right, I *was* longing to get back home – in particular to the privacy of my own room.)

So now it's all down to me. I've got a right to see Chantal and however much our parents continue to screw things up, I want to be sure that we won't end up needing a grotty old fur coat to remind us that one way or another we're sisters.

The Bridegroom

Jamila Gavin

'Muni!' I saw a bird last night!'

'You did, Didi?'

My dear, sweet, youngest sister immediately stopped what she was doing and turned to me.

'Not now, Muni – don't go listening to her crazy dreams now,' begged my middle sister, Tara. 'We'll be late for school.' She pushed me aside and dragged Muni into the kitchen where mother was preparing breakfast.

I began to wail. I couldn't help it. That's me. I show everything. When I'm happy, I jump and shriek and the strangest sounds squawk from my throat, and when I'm sad, I just stand there with my feet apart and hands outstretched like some kind of stone statue, and it's like a river bursts behind my eyes, and other strange noises seem to rise from the very pit of my stomach and force my mouth wide open into an appalling grimace, so I look like some frightful temple demon – at least that's how Tara describes me.

Tara hates me. She sees me as the obstacle to her happiness. The trouble is – she's right. I am an obstacle. You see, I'm the eldest girl, and until I'm married, my younger sisters can't marry. And who'll marry me? I blight the whole family. Everybody whispers. People call me the idiot child. They say my parents must have been bad in their previous life to have had me. So no one wants to be associated with any of us. They're afraid they will be contaminated – and their seed also. I often hear my mother wailing, 'We'll never get any offers for our daughters. They'll never marry – not even our beautiful Tara. Oh, what did I do to deserve this!'

Things went wrong when I was born – perhaps even before I was born. My mother nearly died having me – and then when she saw my large head and squashed up face, and small eyes like a pig, and huge nose like the start of an elephant's trunk, she thrust me away and wouldn't look at me for a month. Then she went to her guru, Narashima, and he warned her that she must have done something very bad in her past life and that I was a test; that if she wanted to be reborn better next time round, she must love and care for me as her most precious child. So she did. She tried as hard as she could. She turned towards me and from then on, never stinted in her devotion. Trouble is, devotion isn't love, and such artificial devotion was a terrible strain on her. Now she has become depressed, withdrawn and wan and sometimes can't get up in the morning and I know it's my fault.

Tara was born almost a year after me – another daughter. Mother and father felt doubly cursed until it gradually became apparent how beautiful she was. Sadly, it didn't affect the situation. People admired Tara and marvelled at her beauty, but there was no rush to make offers of marriage. Muni was born two years after Tara. A third daughter; pretty, too – though not like Tara. My father was disgusted; another girl? Was he not man enough to produce sons? He hardly bothered coming home from the office after that, and when he did, he would be blind drunk and we all had to watch out.

No – I had jinxed the whole family, and everything that went wrong, from the curdling of the milk to my father failing to get promoted, was all my fault.

When Tara was old enough, mother used to beseech her to play with me. But Tara would kick me and pinch me to make me cry. She knew my crying got on Papa's nerves and that sooner or later he would come and shake me and tell me to shut up. I think I'd be dead now, from a broken heart, if it weren't for chota baby – my littlest, sweetest Muni. My life changed when she was born. Now I had a purpose. I carried her about when she was helpless; I fed her and bathed her; I saw her take her first steps and was ready to catch her when she toppled over. It was to me she came when she wanted a cuddle, and it was me she wanted to put her to bed. And as she grew older, she loved me all the more. She doesn't see my ugliness. No complications; no sense of duty, no persuasion to be nice to me – she just loves me. When she was tiny, she used to have nightmares and scream. It was I who used to go to her, quick as a flash. I would gather her up in my arms and rock her and rock her until she fell asleep again. Sometimes I would crawl into bed with her.

But these days, I too have nightmares, dreams which can send me whirling round the house in a kind of madness, and now she does for me what I did for her – she takes my hand and murmurs softly, 'It's all right, Didi. You're safe at home.' And she'll crawl into bed with me. Papa calls us Beauty and the Beast – and there's no kindness in his voice when he says it.

But Muni and I, we always tell each other our

dreams. It became a habit. If I could just tell Muni my dream, and she tell me hers, then I could tolerate the rest of the day, for she would always have an explanation for our dreams.

So there I was wailing at the top of my voice because Tara had dragged Muni away before I could tell her about the bird, and it was important. Very important. So I screamed even louder. 'Muni! Come and listen to my dream.'

Muni came, a piece of toast in her mouth and one arm inside her blazer sleeve while she struggled with the other.

'Quick, Didi, tell me. The school bus will soon be here.'

'There was a bird, Muni. A huge bird.' I pressed my mouth right up to her ear and whispered, 'And I think he's coming for me, not Tara!'

'What are you saying about me?' demanded Tara barging between us and pushing me roughly aside.

'And Muni!' I tried to go on and tell her how I felt about the strange terror and excitement this dream stirred in me, but outside, the school bus blasted its horn impatiently.

'Tell me when I get home,' she cried.

As Tara dragged her off to the bus I could hear Tara begging Muni to tell her what I had been saying about her. Then the bus revved up and shot off down the road in a cloud of dust.

I stared after it for a long time, until it had become just a speck in the distance. Where the road disappeared into the sky, there hung a huge black monsoon cloud, and my dream came back to me all the more vividly. Yes, I had dreamt of a bird – a night bird, longer than the road. It had come flying out of the pitch black depths of monsoon clouds into a moon-struck, ocean sky, where the stars bobbed like fishing boats. The bird was still far away in the distance, its body seeming to stretch far behind it into the milky way. It was beautiful, yet I was frightened, because its neck was as dark blue as Lord Shiva's, and spiralled like the eye of a tornado, sucking everything up in its path.

Strangest of all – and I *tried* to tell Muni – was that on the end of its outstretched neck was a head. 'It's important, Muni,' I whimpered, 'it had a face, and it was flying straight towards me . . .' My voice trailed away as the bus disappeared from sight.

Why had I said it was coming for me not Tara? Was it because Tara is as beautiful as a goddess, and this face was as handsome and noble as a god prince? That all the men who ever came to our house only had eyes for Tara? And yet, I was sure that, in my dream, it was me he was flying to . . . I could hardly admit such a silly idea.

Now I heard the servants whispering. 'Tara has a secret lover. Thinks we don't know . . .' they sniggered triumphantly. 'We know everything. Of course, the boy's family won't let him marry her – not with that elephant-headed sister of hers. If they'd been sensible, they would have smothered her at birth.'

I fled from their horrible talk; horrible, horrible . . . I wanted to run to mother and beg her to comfort me and tell me she loved me and tell her not to worry because everything would be all right when the bird came. But it was no use; when I peered into her bedroom, she was lying like a corpse with her head covered by the sheet, snoring with every breath. 'Mummy!' I whispered, but there was no alteration in the rhythm of her breathing.

I had the same dream again the following night. The same bird, but nearer; that is, its head was nearer but its body still stretched behind all feathery and breaking up into stars as it merged into the land sky of the far distance. I looked into its face, a human face but with the eyes and beak of an eagle. Suddenly the bird fixed one of its eyes on me, a pale, hazel eye, and it was like being pierced by an arrow. I was filled with terror at the sight of it, yet at the same time had such feelings of . . . love? Could I fall in love?

I awoke, throbbing with disturbances and unexplained excitement.

'Muni!' I lumbered clumsily straight into my sister's bed through the pitch of the night, babbling incoherently. 'The bird! He's coming closer. He is coming to claim me. I'm frightened. Will he kill me or embrace me – I can't tell.'

Muni rolled in her sleep, muttering comforting words and hugged me close. 'Don't worry, Didi – it's only a dream. It won't hurt you. It's only a bird.'

'No, Muni – it has a man's face – it looks at me so lovingly and I know it's coming to marry me.'

That made Muni wake up. 'Marry you, Didi? Marry *you*?'

For a horrible moment, I thought she was going to laugh – just as Tara would have laughed, or mother would have sighed, or father would have thrown up his eyes in despair. My breath halted in my lungs; I stopped breathing; if she laughed . . . if she laughed . . .

But she didn't. She murmured softly, 'But that's wonderful, Didi, I always knew someone would come for you one day.'

'Yet I'm afraid, Muni. No one but you loves me. Everyone else just sees my ugliness.'

'Perhaps your dream bird sees you as I do, the most beautiful person in the world. Of course it loves you.'

I lay there wondering. But can I love? Tara doesn't think so. Tara doesn't see me as human with human feelings. Because no man will ever love me, she thinks I'm incapable of love. But I have my fantasies too. Everyone thinks that because I'm ugly I don't dream of having a wonderful lover; that I don't yearn for a man to circle the flame with me in marriage. I tell Muni about it – and oh how we laugh together and tell each other stories about handsome princes who come riding in chariots, begging for our hands in marriage – and all the time with an ache in our hearts for it seems that it can never be – and all because of me.

The next day there was no school. Mother and Tara went shopping, so that meant they would be away for hours. As usual, Muni was happy to stay with me and oh, how she teased me about my dream bird. 'Your prince is coming to carry you away for ever. Come on, let's play dressing up. I want to dress you as a bride – from top to bottom. Just to show you how it will be when your day comes.'

'Oh, Muni,' I giggled, though I wanted to cry. 'My day will never come.'

'Nonsense,' exclaimed Muni dramatically. 'You're magic. You see. Only the most special perfect magic person will find you, and then he'll take you away – and . . .'

'And then you and Tara will be free to marry!' I cried.

Muni was bursting with excitement. She rushed into

our mother's room and began raiding her wardrobe. She found mother's scarlet and gold wedding saree, and all her jewellery; gold rings for the fingers and toes, golden bangles, chains, earrings and necklaces; pearls for the hair, mascara and charcoal for my eyes, lipstick and henna for my lips and skin. She gathered it all together and then set about turning me into a bride.

By the time mother and Tara came home, it was getting dark, but just as we heard the wheels of the car crunching up the drive, Muni finished the last intricate coil of her design in henna on my hands. She sat back on her heels, suddenly exhausted. She had worked so hard. But there I was, looking like a bride, glowing in the crimson saree, glittering with the jewels, my piggy eyes looking round and dark and almost big, outlined as they were with the charcoal, and my lashes swept upwards with mascara. Muni had woven pearls into my hair, outlined my parting in red; my ears and neck gleamed with rubies and gold, making my skin reflect like honey, and in my elephant nose shone a diamond stud. I stared at myself in the mirror, not daring to move. Was that me, really me?

'Oh, Didi, you look beautiful!' breathed Muni, amazed at the transformation.

'What on earth!' a harsh voice lacerated our fantasy. 'Mummy! Just *look* what Muni and Didi have been up to!' Tara's voice was shrill with scorn and indignation.

'Oh no! Not my wedding saree! Not my very best saree! How could you!'

I felt a ringing stinging slap.

Muni began to whimper. 'Don't hit Didi. It isn't her fault. I made her do it. I wanted her to look beautiful – like a bride. We haven't done any harm.'

Muni's hand reached out for mine, but was dragged from my clasp and I began to shake.

'Make her look beautiful? Like a bride? What kind of stupid ideas have you been putting in her head?'

Mother and Tara raged and sneered in turn, and made such a hullaballoo that even the servants came running.

Then from outside came a dreadful whistling sound. A whistling which became a rumbling which grew louder and louder and louder. The electric lights dipped crazily in and out and finally out. We were plunged into darkness.

Voices were yelling, 'What's happening?'

'It's a storm coming.'

'More like a tornado,' shouted my father's voice, high with alarm.

'Look, look at the sky . . . What is that!'

My mother and sisters ran outside to see, leaving me still dressed as a bride, staring through the window at the unimaginable sky.

It was my dream, my bird. I could see his great, long body – trailing with clouds and stars and feathery plumes trickling like waterfalls, streaming behind him, spreading across the whole moonlit sky. I could see his dark blue throat twisting and sucking, as if he consumed the universe. Nearer and nearer he came, and now I saw that hazel eye fixed on me and suddenly he was everywhere. I braced myself for pain. I would be drowned, smothered, knocked to the ground, battered and stripped.

I felt something grip my wrist. A grip from which I could never escape; an eagle's talon with claws of steel, yet as light as a bangle which leaves not one scratch on my skin. I am being lifted; taken; claimed; carried away. All solid things dissolve. I am simply absorbed into light and time and space. I look down on my home and parents and sisters.

Oh, Muni, my dearest sweet younger sister, I can see you running desperately back into the house; running and screaming in terror as you burst into the room where you dressed me as a bride – and you do not find me. You spin in circles, blinded with hysteria, and I beg you to calm down and realise what has happened; that you were right. My prince has come – and you are all free. At last, as you fall weeping to the ground, your hand touches a feather. You look up and the room is floating with feathers and now you know.

About the Authors

Joanna Carey
I think now, after bringing up my own three boys, I'd appreciate the company of a sister but as a child that was the last thing I wanted. I wasn't an only child like Daveen in my story, but I really did enjoy the freedom – and the privacy – of the rather solitary position I held as the youngest in the family, and the only girl.

Helen Dunmore
You can't get away from your sisters, even if you want to. It's a close, challenging, enduring relationship that takes a lifetime to understand. My last novel, *Talking to the Dead*, was about love and tragedy between two sisters.

Anne Fine
When we are young, we simply accept our homes, and those with whom we share them. But then a kind of questioning creeps in, and, with it, judgement. Which sisterly relations survive this process, and which don't tell us, I think, a good deal more about ourselves and what we think important than they will ever tell us about these so known – and so *un*known – members of our own families.

Other books by Anne Fine which include sibling relationships are: *The Granny Project, Madame Doubtfire, Goggle-Eyes, The Book of the Banshee* and *Step by Wicked Step*.

Jamila Gavin
Nothing is worse than the enmity of sisters; nothing is better than sisterhood. The *Surya Trilogy* is important to me because I was able to explore many of the themes I find absorbing – including, in *Track of the Wind* – the relationship of sisters.

Maeve Henry
When I was growing up no one was closer to me than my older sister and no one could make me quite so angry. Unshakeably loyal, she strove to dominate, cajole and teach me while I resented and depended on her. Our relationship now still reflects that childhood wrangling. We talk deeply but hardly ever admit our love in words. My book, *A Summer Dance*, explores the relationship between two sisters.

Lynne Markham
The relationship between sisters is a complex one; it has to withstand

comparison, competition, envy, but it can also provide security, warmth and a sense of belonging. Who else has known you all your life? As you get older you value that continuity and the old cliché rings true – blood *is* thicker than water, after all.

Jenny Nimmo
Many of my earlier books (the *Snow Spider Trilogy* and *Ultramarine*) were coloured by the fact that I was an only child. It led me to believe that siblings were very special to each other, and although my own children tried to disabuse me of this, I still believe that my life would have been all the better for a sister.

Jacqueline Wilson
I am an only child but I always longed for a sister. Sometimes I write about children like me (*Tracy Beaker*) or children with step-siblings (Andy in *The Suitcase Kid* and Elsa in *The Bed and Breakfast Star*) and *Double Act* dealt with an intense relationship between twin sisters. It was a delightful challenge to come up with a new twist on the sister theme for this super anthology!

Diana Wynne Jones
When I think of my sisters, the first thing that occurs to me is loyalty. To this day, we all back one another up all the time. I find I put this in my books without questioning it – for instance, *Power of Three*, where Anya, Gair and Ceri form a solid small group against a very frightening world. The second thing is probably responsibility, which is mostly mine. As the eldest I had almost sole charge of my sisters from an early age and I never would have dreamt of dumping them on someone else like the eldest sisters is *The Girl Jones*. I looked after them the way Renata does in *The Magicians of Caprona* or Sophie in *Howl's Moving Castle*, or even Howard in *Archer's Goon*. The third thing I think of when I think of my sisters, is laughter. We ring one another up and reduce each other to tears of mirth, with the sort of mad, logical humour that comes in *The Ogre Downstairs*. This is not to say we don't quarrel. Some of the quarrels in *The Time of the Ghost*, *The Spellcoats* and *Cart and Cwidder* were drawn from life. And there are always times when, as a writer, I find that things have grown thin and grey and I'm not sure where what I'm writing is going; and then one of my sisters phones, as if she knew, and will make everything come alive again by saying just one simple thing – usually wholly unexpected. I think I am very lucky in my sisters.